Other titles by Steve Barlow and Steve Skidmore

Tales of the Dark Forest

1. Goodknyght!
2. Whizzard
4. Knyghtmare!

The Lost Diary of...

Erik Bloodaxe, Viking Warrior
Hercules' Personal Trainer
Shakespeare's Ghostwriter
Robin Hood's Money Man
King Henry VIII's Executioner
Julius Caesar's Slave

TALES OF THE DARK FOREST

TROLLOGY!

STEVE BARLOW & STEVE SKIDMORE

ILLUSTRATED BY FIONA LAND

HarperCollins *Children's Books*

First published in Great Britain by HarperCollins *Children's Books* in 2003
HarperCollins *Children's Books* is a division of HarperCollins*Publishers* Ltd,
77-85 Fulham Palace Road, Hammersmith,
London, W6 8JB

3

ISBN-13 978 0 00 710865 7
ISBN-10 0 00 710865 6

Printed and bound in England by
Clays Ltd, St Ives plc

The Legend of the Dark Forest

According to legend, the Dark Forest was not always dark. Long ago, the Kings of the Forest ruled a rich and fertile land from their high throne in the great City of Dun Indewood. Their prosperous and peaceful realm was defended by brave and honourable Knyghts, and you couldn't throw a rock without hitting a beautiful maiden, a sturdy forester or a rosy, apple-cheeked farmer. (Of course, none of the contented citizens of Dun Indewood would ever dream of throwing rocks about anyway; and if they did, one of the Knyghts, who were not only brave and honourable but just and kindly too, would ask them very politely not to do it again.)

It was a Golden Age.

But over the years, the Knyghts and Lords of the City grew greedy, idle and dishonest, and fell to quarrelling among themselves. The line of the Kings died out.

The power of Dun Indewood declined. Contact with the other cities and towns that lay in the vast wilderness of the Dark Forest became rare, and then was lost altogether when the Forest roads became too dangerous to travel.

The creatures of the Forest became wild and dangerous until only a few hardy souls dared to brave its perils. The citizens of Dun Indewood continued to argue among themselves and cheat each other, turning their backs on everything that happened outside the City walls.

With no one to tame it, the Forest became home to truly dreadful things. Beasts with the understanding of men, and men with the ferocity of beasts, roamed the dark paths. The trees themselves became malevolent and watchful. And the Forest grew...

Well, that's the legend, anyway.

Of course, these days, nobody believes a word of it...

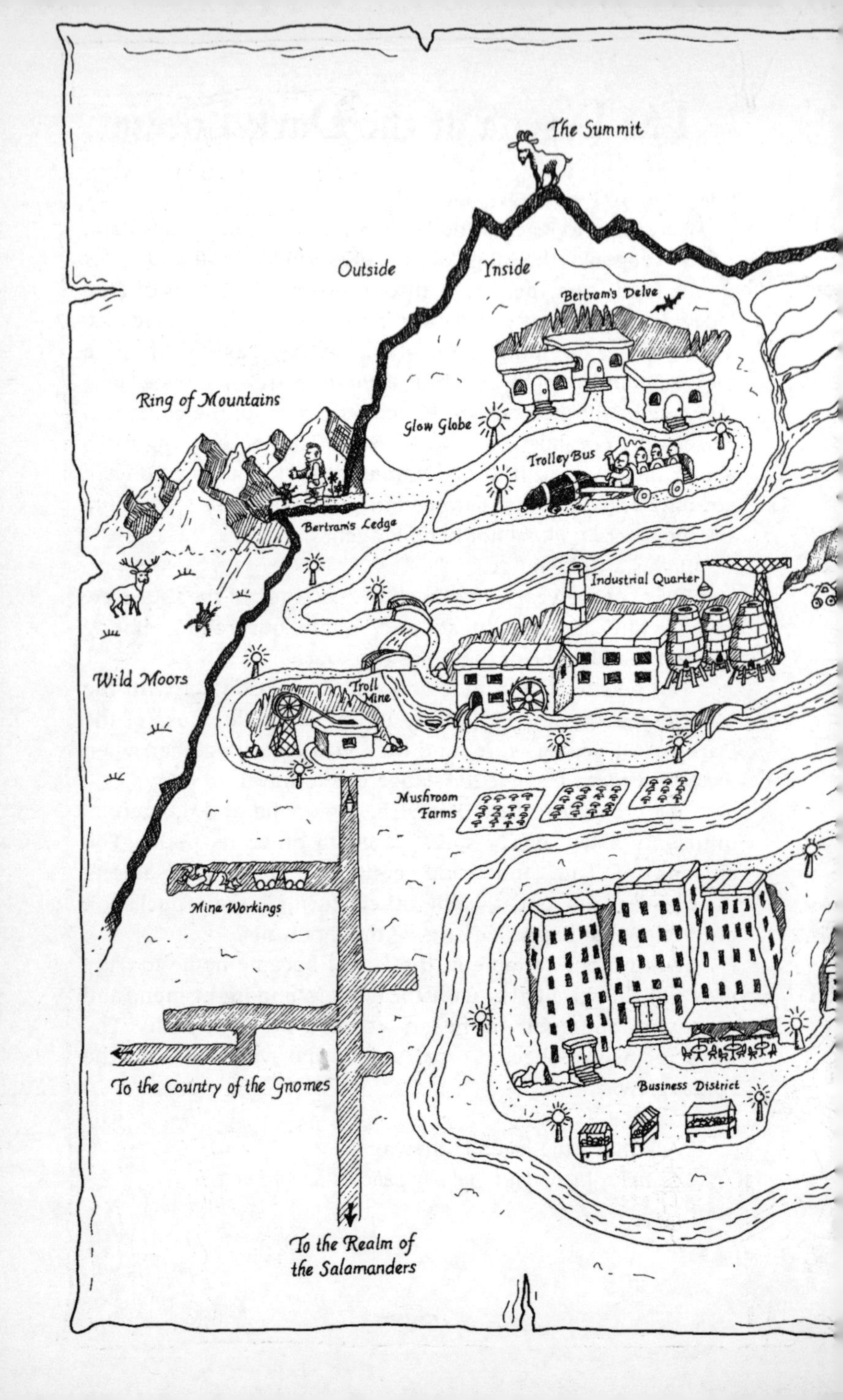
The Summit
Outside
Ynside
Bertram's Delve
Ring of Mountains
Glow Globe
Trolley Bus
Bertram's Ledge
Industrial Quarter
Wild Moors
Troll Mine
Mushroom Farms
Mine Workings
To the Country of the Gnomes
Business District
To the Realm of the Salamanders

The City of
Caer Borundum
beneath
Mount Ynside
Up
Greystone Park
Troll
Grotto
Lake
Bandstand
Old
Quarry
Secret Excavations
Suburbs
The Rock
Lovers'
Plummet
Trollmoot
Hall
Ironstone Square
Councillor Shale's
House
The
Trollenbach
Falls

Book The First

The Book of the Trolls

(The Fellowship of the Lemming)

Chapter One

How Bertram met a Lemming who Looked before he Leapt.

High on the slopes of Mount Ynside, Bertram Hornblende clasped his callused hands behind his head and lay back, enjoying the warmth of the sun on his face.

Out of the corner of his eye, he saw a brownish blur as something small and furry raced past him and leapt off the ledge where he lay, launching itself into empty space.

"Yyyyiiiiiippppppppeeeeeeeeeeeeeeeeeeeee!"

Bertram ignored the intrusion. It was good to be alive, he thought. Above him, wispy clouds flowed across skies patrolled by eagles and hawks, while sable-winged ravens croaked threats and insults at each other as they swooped and squabbled. Hearing the *kwok-kok-kok* call of a wild bird from far below, Bertram looked down from his high ledge to where fleecier clouds drifted softly across the distant landscape of moors that surrounded the mountain.

Another furry streak shot past him.

"Here goes nnnnnnooooottthhhhhhiiinnnnggggggg!"

Behind Bertram, the gigantic flanks of Mount Ynside reached up, scarred by snowfields and glaciers. Its jagged, white-capped peaks seemed to clutch at the sky. From its lower slopes, the barking challenge of a stag echoed across the wild moors. Further down still, the wild grasses and heathers gave way to alpine meadows where goats roamed. The reedy, plaintive notes of their distant bleating trembled in the still air.

A third intruder raced across the ledge and hurled itself into the void.

"Going ddddddoooooowwwwwwwnnnnnnnnnnnnnnn!"

Beyond the meadows lay a forest. The ancient legends of Bertram's people called it the Dark Forest and said that its trees stretched further than the eye could see, an endless world of green. But Bertram did not know whether this was true. He didn't even have a very clear idea of what a tree looked like close to: there were no trees this high up, only stunted bushes and the springy heather that in summer transformed the sombre brown landscape of the high moors into fields of glowing purple.

"Heads bbbeeeeeeellllllllllllllllooooooooooowwwwwwwwww!"

The sun was already dipping towards the western

horizon. Soon it would be time to go home. Bertram closed his eyes – and frowned. His contented mood faded.

Nobody understood him. What was wrong with his friends and neighbours? When Bertram so much as mentioned the outside world they shuddered and looked at him strangely, and made excuses to get away as quickly as they could. Why? It was wonderful out here! Bertram loved the sound of birdsong, and the wind as it rustled through the grass. He loved the sun on his back.

None of this would have been unusual if Bertram had been human. It would have been normal. It would have been expected. But Bertram wasn't human.

Bertram was a troll.

"Goodbye, cruel WWoooorrrrrrrlllllllllddddddddddd!"

Trolls lived in the mountains, in deep, dark, hidden places where currents of air murmured and underground streams thundered. Trolls shrank from the light, but Bertram was scared of the dark. In fact, sunlight was supposed to be deadly to trolls. Any troll caught by the rays of the sun would be instantly turned into stone. All troll children learned this at their mother's knee, but when Bertram had stumbled upon a way to the surface many years ago, he found that the light of the sun merely warmed him. It made him feel alive. Just as it was doing now.

"Gggaaaannnggggwwwwwwwaaaaaaaaayyyyyyy!"

Usually, Bertram enjoyed complete solitude when he ventured above ground from the troll city of Caer Borundum to his ledge on the face of the mountain. It was as close as he ever came to being happy, lying out here with the sun on his face, the coarse grass tickling his back and the world spread out before him. But today, for some reason, the place was teeming with small, furry creatures who, from time to time, insisted on scampering across the ledge where Bertram was sitting (and occasionally across Bertram himself) and flinging themselves to their doom with piercing cries.

"Oh, dearie, dearie me."

Bertram opened his eyes – and blinked.

There in front of him, peering over the edge at the sheer drop below, was one of those small, furry creatures. But this creature didn't look at all happy at the prospect of hurling itself off the ledge. It was muttering to itself in a worried sort of way.

"Right then – one, two, three, and away we go... Or should it be three, two, one? Oh, well, I don't suppose it matters... Then I shout 'Geranium'... no, that's not right. 'Geology'... no, it wasn't that. Oh, well, I daresay I'll remember when the time comes. So it's one, two, three, 'Geometry' or whatever, *and*... plummet! Yes, that seems about right—"

"Excuse me," said Bertram.

The creature gave a startled squeak and spun round to face him. It teetered on the edge of the drop, desperately windmilling its stubby arms to regain its balance. Then it clutched at its chest with one quivering forepaw and bunched the other into a tiny fist, which it shook at Bertram.

"What do you mean, you great clodhopper, sneaking up on me and bellowing like that? You nearly had me over."

"I'm sorry I startled you," said Bertram. "But I didn't sneak up on you, I was here all the time."

"I thought you were a pile of rocks." The creature stared at Bertram with its small, black, near-sighted eyes. "Hang on – you're a troll, aren't you?"

"How did you guess?" asked Bertram wearily.

"Well, what are you doing out here in the day? You're supposed to turn to stone in sunlight, aren't you?"

Bertram shrugged. "That's what they say, but it doesn't seem to happen to me. I don't know why."

The small, furry creature whistled. "*Weird*."

Bertram felt a wave of misery wash over him. He was used to other trolls avoiding him and giving him strange looks – but even this odd creature, which he'd never met before, had spotted straight away that he was different from other trolls. He *must* be weird.

His misery gave way to annoyance. This was *his* ledge. What gave this interloper the right to make personal comments? "What are you doing here?" he demanded.

The creature drew itself up to its full height, and completely failed to look impressive. "If you must know, Mister Weird Troll," it said defiantly, "I'm jumping. Don't try and stop me!"

"Oh," said Bertram. "Do you think that's wise?"

The creature blinked. "Wise?"

"Yes – I mean, it's a sheer drop several hundred feet on to solid rock." Bertram stood up and wandered to the edge of the cliff. "Solid, *jagged* rock. I should think you'd go splat in a pretty final sort of way."

The creature shuddered. "Thank you so much for reminding me. I was trying to put it out of my mind."

Bertram's brow creased. "Then why do you want to jump?"

"Well, I wouldn't say I *want* to," said the creature unhappily. "Not *want* to as such. It's more a case of *having* to." It gave Bertram a look of miserable defiance. "I'm a lemming."

"I see," said Bertram politely, not seeing at all.

"So there you are."

Bertram was nonplussed. "Where am I?"

"I mean, there you have it."

Bertram gave an apologetic shrug. "I'm sorry, I don't understand. What's a lemming?" He looked back at the cleft in the rock behind him that led back to his own world. "I'm afraid I don't get out much."

"Well, that's why I have to jump – because I'm a lemming. Jumping off mountains is what lemmings do." The lemming looked down and gave a little shudder. "I think. I'm pretty sure. Not all the time of course..."

"Only once, I should think."

"I mean, it doesn't happen every year. But every now and again we lemmings get an urge, you see..."

"An urge to find somewhere high up and jump off it?"

"Exactly! And then it's one, two, three, off we go, shout 'Gingerbread' or something on the way down, and..."

"Splat."

"Don't say that!" objected the lemming.

"Why?"

"Because I'm trying not to think about it!"

"No, I mean, why jump?"

The lemming blinked. "Well, I don't know. It's sort of built in. It's something lemmings have to do. It's more or less what we're *for*."

Bertram felt sorry for the unhappy creature. "What's your name?"

The lemming gave him a hard look and said, "Cliff," as if challenging Bertram to make any funny remarks.

Bertram managed to stifle a giggle. "I'm Bertram. You know, Cliff," he went on gently, "I don't suppose you really have to throw yourself off this cli— I mean, ledge. Not if you don't want to."

The lemming looked at him with wistful eyes. "Do you really think so?"

Bertram nodded. "Yes."

For a moment, the lemming was clearly undecided. He looked at the drop before him. He looked back at Bertram. Then he looked at the drop again. He steeled himself – and turned to glare at Bertram as if the whole situation were his fault.

"Oh, yes? Oh, yes?" The lemming stamped one tiny foot. "What would you know about it, anyway? How can I be a proper lemming if I don't hurl myself off this ledge? Answer me that! Do you think I want to go down in history as 'Cliff, The Lemming Who Wouldn't Jump'?"

Bertram looked down sadly at the furious little creature. Despite their physical differences, he was beginning to feel that he and Cliff were remarkably similar. They were both unable to live up to what was expected of them.

"How would you like that, eh? To be different, everyone pointing at you, whispering about you, mothers telling their children, 'Don't you go talking to *him*, he's not a proper lemming. He's different. He's *strange*'."

Bertram sighed and turned his back on Cliff. He collected the bunch of flowers he had picked earlier in the day and began to amble away.

"Anyway, I'm not in the mood now, so there!" scolded the lemming. "You've ruined the moment. I was all ready to go and you went and spoiled it. I hope you're satisfied." Cliff scowled at Bertram's retreating back and dusted his paws. "That told him!" he muttered to himself. "Well, it's too late to do anything now. I'll just have to come back tomorrow."

"Evening!"

Cliff turned. Another lemming was trotting briskly towards the cliff edge, with a cheery smile on its furry face. It peered over the edge and took in the view with an appreciative nod. "Jumping, are you? Nice day for it."

Cliff took a step back. "Yes, absolutely – ah – just taking a look at the terrain, you know, pacing out my run-up, things like that." The other lemming raised its eyebrows. "I mean, we only get one shot at this, don't we? I'd hate to get it wrong."

"Oh, quite! Mind you, there's a lot to be said for just getting on with it, don't you think? No point in hanging about. In fact, would you mind awfully if I went first?"

Cliff hastily stood aside. "No, no – not at all, be my guest."

"Jolly decent of you." The second lemming balanced on its toes at the edge of the gulf and raised its heels off the ground three times. Then it took a deep breath, held its nose and hurled itself into empty space with a cry of "Geronniiimmmmmmooooooooooooo!"

"Oh, yes, 'Geronimo'," Cliff muttered sadly. "That's the word." He inched forward until he could see over the edge to the rocks far below and shuddered. "Yes, I'll come back tomorrow, definitely," he decided. "Or the next day. Or maybe the day after that. There's no rush."

Bertram caught nothing of this exchange. On hearing the reedy, distant cry of the plummeting lemming behind him, he paused by the fissure that led back into the heart of the mountain. Poor Cliff had obviously lost the struggle against his instincts and leapt to his doom. The troll looked down at the flowers he held in his great fist and shook his head sadly.

On the opposite side of the valley, the sun touched the treetops of the distant Forest and lit the slowly drifting clouds with a blaze of gold. As it slipped from the sky and the shadows of dusk claimed the mountainside, Bertram stepped from the world of light back into the dark kingdom of the trolls.

Chapter Two

Of Crumbly Cakes, Larks in the Park and a Stroll with a Troll.

"They aren't hard enough!" groaned Bertram. He stared unhappily at the dozen squishy mounds on the baking tray he'd just removed from the oven. Bertram sighed, picked up a well-worn recipe-slate and checked the instructions again:

MRS BEETEM'S TOOTH BUSTING ROCKE CAKES

INGREEDYUNTS

2 poundes of finest grit
8 ownces of batter
1 pounde of pebbles (medium size)
a fistefulle of rock salte

COOKINIT

Batter the batter. Grind the grit. Pound in the pebbles. Chuck in the salt. Stir with finger. Shove in the oven. Take out when cooked.

Where had he gone wrong? The recipe seemed simple enough. All troll recipes were simple, the simplest being that for Cold Rock (*Pick up rock. Eat it.*). But in general, even trolls preferred their rocks a bit more digestible, so they baked refined grit into loaves, bannocks – and rock cakes. Troll teeth were capable of munching almost anything softer than quartz, and they preferred their rock cakes on the crunchy side. But Bertram simply couldn't seem to manage this – his cakes always had a melt-in-your-mouth crumbliness that trolls found disgusting, and this latest batch was no different.

His mother looked up from the slate she was working on, one of several spread across the kitchen table. "Is something the matter?" she asked vaguely.

Bertram raked the ash from the bottom of the firebox and poured it over the glowing coals to damp them down. Then he picked up the tray of soggy cakes. "I followed the recipe," he said mournfully. "I even washed my finger before I stirred the mixture."

Pumice Hornblende peered at the cakes in an unfocused sort of way. "They look lovely," she said unconvincingly.

Bertram shook his head. "They're far too soft."

His mother smiled bravely and picked up one of Bertram's creations. She nibbled it delicately and immediately went into a coughing fit.

"Lovely," she repeated, her eyes watering.

Bertram regarded her sadly. She tried hard, but motherhood came to Pumice about as easily as being a "normal" troll came to Bertram. She was Keeper of the Slates at the Caer Borundum Library. It was her job to decipher all the worn-out, cracked, chipped or incomplete slates on which the ancient knowledge of the trolls was inscribed. Bertram suspected that the world of the past was a lot more real to his mother than the one in which she actually lived.

She gave Bertram a tremulous smile. "You really have a talent, Bertram. How many boy-trolls can cook? And not every troll can bake soft rock cakes."

No other troll would want to, thought Bertram. But he just said, "Thanks, Mum."

"Anyway," continued Pumice, "why all this cooking?" She gave Bertram a conspiratorial wink. "Are those cakes a little present for someone?"

Bertram cringed inwardly and a blue flush spread across his face.

"And would that someone just happen to be Councillor Shale's niece Opal?"

"Mum!" Bertram protested. Pumice gave a delighted laugh.

Bertram had known Opal Drumlin since they were troddlers. Opal was in Bertram's class at Doctor Chalk's Academy. Bertram had a soft spot for Opal: the whole of his brain turned to mud whenever he saw her (which caused all sorts of problems in class). Opal's uncle was one of the richest and most important trolls in Caer Borundum.

Fortunately, Councillor Shale seemed to like Bertram – and so, for some unfathomable reason, did Opal.

Bertram's mother smiled and patted him on the shoulder. "I'm sure she'll think they're delicious." She glanced up at the water clock on the stone dresser. "Goodness, is that the time? I must go." She bustled about, gathering up her slates and packing them into a moleskin bag. "Are you staying in this evening, dear?"

Bertram steeled himself. "I thought I'd go out," he said offhandedly. "I said I'd meet Opal, in the park."

His mother stopped packing and gave him an unhappy look. "All right, dear," she said slowly, "but you won't be out late, will you? One hears such dreadful things. You will be here when I get back?"

Bertram sighed inwardly. "Yes, Mum." He hated it when his mother fussed like this. But he knew why. She had lost Bertram's father before Bertram had been born. She didn't want to lose Bertram as well.

"Good. Well, I must be off."

"Mum," said Bertram. As Pumice paused at the door, he struggled to put into words the thought that had been nagging him ever since he had met Cliff the lemming. "Why am I weird?"

A concerned look flashed across his mother's face. "Why do you say that?"

Bertram sighed. "Like you said, other boy-trolls don't cook. They like fighting and I don't. I collect flowers, they collect rocks. I can't tell chalk from basalt. I wouldn't know a coarse-grained igneous rock if it fell on me. Every other troll *knows* these things!" Bertram shook his head. "And why am I the only troll in the whole of Caer Borundum who can go into the outside world in daylight without being turned into a statue? I *must* be weird!"

"Bertram..." His mother took a step forward, a look of distress on her face. Then she stopped and spread her hands helplessly. "I must go. Try not to worry." She fumbled with the door latch.

Sighing again, Bertram went to his bedroom and combed his crest. He took a bottle of after-scrape lotion (*Tunnel No 5 – Essence pour Troll*) from the back of a drawer where, he hoped, his mother wouldn't find it. He shook a few drops into his hands, which he patted over his face. Then he returned to the kitchen and carefully packed the cakes into a spider-web basket. He picked up the bunch of flowers he'd gathered in the outside world, took a deep breath and headed for the door.

Bertram flagged down the trolleybus in the tunnel outside his home. The driver hauled on his reins to bring the draught-moles to a stop. These massive, deep-chested creatures (distant relatives of the small, surface-dwelling mammals) had been bred by the trolls for strength and stamina. Blind and patient, the moles waited while Bertram got on the bus; then, at the driver's command of "Waggons mole!", they heaved the clumsy iron vehicle into motion and set off down the tunnel.

The bus was crowded and full of the cheery buzz of voices – which faded as Bertram got on. Several pairs of eyes watched as he made his way to an empty seat. When the conversation started up again, it was subdued. Bertram sat clutching his flowers and bag of cakes, trying unsuccessfully to make himself inconspicuous.

Other trolls didn't know what to make of Bertram. He worried them. These days he'd given up even trying to be friendly – all he ever got were blank looks or polite, dismissive replies.

Bertram stared out of the window. The bus was passing a mine where a mournful hooter signalled a change of shift. Hundreds of small figures, covered in rock dust, streamed out of the gate. These were picksies, who lived and worked alongside trolls in the mines. Picksies were civil and kept themselves to themselves. Trolls generally paid them about as much attention as they paid Bertram, which made him feel a certain warmth towards the long-nosed little miners.

The trolleybus rumbled on, through the industrial areas of Caer Borundum. It passed the mills whose huge, creaking paddle wheels, turned by water from the Troll River, powered the giant grindstones that pulverised rock from the mines into grit. It passed the foundries and forges, where fires glowed white, red and orange as they smelted and shaped iron for the city. It passed the fungus fields, where pallid mushrooms and toadstools grew, glowing faintly in the darkness, and the battery farms, where bats were reared to supply Caer Borundum's message service (and much of its food).

As it entered the heart of the city, the trolleybus bowled past the library, the repository of all the history and legends of the trolls. In her small office on the second floor, Bertram's mother would by now be poring over more crumbling and faded records, and translating their contents into modern Trollish.

Bertram got off the bus at the entrance to Greystone Park and walked through the great stone gates. Iron glow-posts lined the gravel walkways, their phosphorescent globes casting a pale luminescence over the grounds.

Most trolls thought Greystone Park was the most beautiful and romantic place in the whole of Caer Borundum, but its beauty was lost on Bertram. How could the gravel pathways, cave-moss lawns and algae water-gardens compare to the flowers, grasses and marsh plants of the outer world? What were the bats of the caverns to the birds of the open sky, or the crystal outcrops and carved rock faces to the mountain peaks, snowfields and glaciers? He longed to share it all with Opal, but he knew that was impossible.

He passed by the lake and the huge basalt rock formation known as the Trolls' Causeway, and turned right, heading towards the bandstand where he hoped Opal would be waiting.

She wasn't. Bertram groaned. Opal was nowhere to be seen – but her friends Beryl, Garnet and Topaz were sitting on the iron rails of the bandstand. As if that weren't enough, next to the girls stood their boyfriends: Clay, Marlstone and Greywacke. Their deep grunts of laughter filled the air.

Bertram decided to turn back before they spotted him, but he was too late.

"Whaddaya know, it's Bertram!"

Bertram protested feebly as he was troll-handled into the middle of the bandstand where the young trolls surrounded him, leering. He knew what was coming next.

"I say, I say, I say," said Marlstone. "What's softer than talc?"

"I dunno," replied Clay, "What *is* softer than talc?"

"Bertram!"

Roars of laughter rose from the bandstand.

"What's big and grey and afraid of the dark?"

"A very old mole?"

"No – Bertram!" More laughter.

"What's all soppy, wet and drippy?"

"An underground lake?"

"No."

"A soppy, wet, drippy thing?"

"No. Give up?"

"No, wait, don't tell me, let me guess... it must be... Bertram!"

"Oh, har-de-har," said Bertram unhappily.

Beryl sniffed. "Why haven't you got a proper troll name? Something to do with rocks, or minerals, like normal trolls have," she sneered. "I mean, what sort of name is Bertram? Sounds kinda human to me."

A lone, dissenting voice cut through the jeers. "It's Bertram's name." Opal stepped up on to the bandstand. "Hi, Bertram. Sorry I'm late."

Bertram had never been so glad to see Opal. As usual, his brain began to turn mushy. Heedless of Opal's friends, Bertram held out his bunch of flowers. "I picked these for you, Opal..."

"Flowers!" screeched Beryl. "You've been Out There again! Yeuch! Bertram, you are such a sump-head!"

Bertram groaned inwardly. His visits to his ledge weren't a secret (it was almost impossible to keep secrets in the enclosed world of Caer Borundum), but Bertram seemed to get into trouble every time he mentioned them or brought anything back from the world outside.

"Couldn't you have got Opal a nice crystal instead?" demanded Beryl. Garnet and Topaz nodded vigorously in agreement. "Don't you know that diamonds are a troll's best friend?"

Opal gave Beryl a hard stare. "Speak for yourself. I don't care what you think, *I* like flowers..." But before she could take the offered gift, Marlstone had snatched it.

"So do I!" he roared, stuffing the flowers into his mouth. "To eat!" Greywacke and Clay guffawed and Beryl, Garnet and Topaz tittered as Bertram looked on helplessly.

Marlstone spat out the mangled remains of Bertram's gift. "Why don't you go down into the deep caverns and bring Opal a nice gemstone, *Bertie*? What's the matter – are you scared of the dark?"

Opal placed her hands on her hips and stared hard at Marlstone. "Why don't you go to the outside world to pick some flowers for Beryl, *Marlie*? What's the matter – are you scared of the light?"

Marlstone glowered at her. "No. Only an idiot would go outside for a few bits of weed!"

Opal crossed the bandstand and took Bertram's arm. "Well, I think flowers are romantic. And I think Bertram is very brave."

"Brave!" shrilled Topaz. "He's just weird!"

Bertram blinked. There was that word again – weird!

Marlstone gave Opal an angry look. "Have it your way." He took Beryl's hand and spun her round. "Come on, you trollops!" (Bertram winced – his mother thought "trollop" was a rude way to refer to a troll girl.) "Let's get down and go dancing in the dark," Marlstone continued. "*The Ministry of Stone* has got some top headbangers on tonight. It should be rockin'!"

Topaz nodded. "If Opal doesn't want to come, leave her with the weirdo. She'll soon see sense."

Beryl, Topaz and Garnet took their partners' arms. With an orchestrated "humph!", they swept off, noses in the air.

"They're right, you know." Bertram leant on the rail of the bandstand and watched the retreating group. "I *am* weird. I'm totally different from every other troll in Caer Borundum, so I must be."

"Shut up, Bertram," ordered Opal. "You are not weird. Just ignore those dip-slips." She gave Bertram a cheerful grin and skipped down the steps of the bandstand, pointing to a large opening in a nearby rock face. "The Troll Grotto!" she cried. "Let's go in there!"

She led Bertram through the black cleft. As they went

down a series of steps carved into the rock, the narrow passage opened out before them into a huge cavern. The sight that met their eyes was stunning. Hundreds of stalactites hung down from the ceiling like coloured icicles, mirrored by stalagmites reaching up to join with their hanging companions. The cavern walls sparkled in rainbow-hued patterns. Opal led Bertram over to a shimmering outcrop of quartz. "Isn't it glorious? The way these crystals light up the whole cavern."

They sat down on a seat carved from rock salt. Opal pointed at the veins of minerals that jutted out through the rock walls in a kaleidoscope of colour and began to name them. "There's malachite over there – see? And galena, quartz, calcite – and have you ever seen such beautiful feldspars?"

Bertram stared at the cavern walls in dumb misery. Troll eyes were supposed to be able to distinguish between different rock and mineral types, formations and gemstones. But Bertram was stone-blind. He couldn't tell chalk from china clay, lava from limestone or schist from a hole in the ground.

"Isn't it romantic?" said Opal, snuggling closer to Bertram. He gulped and felt his stomach tighten.

"What's your favourite rock, Bertram?"

Bertram gestured helplessly. "I can't tell one ore from another. Doctor Chalk said I got the lowest mark ever recorded in the Orenithology exam. You see all that stuff – silicates and micas and quartz; all I see is rock."

Opal went quiet and pulled away from Bertram. There

was a long silence and Bertram cursed inwardly. He should have lied – pretended to admire all the structures and colours he couldn't see. In an attempt to remedy the situation, he reached into his bag and pulled out the cakes. "I made you these."

Opal stared apprehensively at the oddly shaped lumps. "For me?"

Bertram nodded nervously.

"What are they?"

"Rock cakes."

"You're kidding." Opal caught herself as she sensed Bertram's disappointment. "Oh, *rock* cakes! Right! Of course they're rock cakes. What else could they be?" She took one and nibbled at it, as Bertram's mother had done. Her smile froze.

"Don't you like them?" asked Bertram.

"Well," said Opal, trying not to spit out the cake, "they're a little soft..."

"I know," said Bertram glumly. "I followed the recipe, but they just came out weird. Like me." He slumped on the seat.

Opal took his hand in a fierce grip. "Bertram Hornblende," she said sternly, "I don't care if other trolls think you're weird. *I* don't think you are. You're just different from all the others." She gave an exasperated snort. "Don't you get it, you dumb troll? I like you *because* you're different..."

Bertram stared at her in astonishment and reawakened hope. His heart began to beat at an alarming rate. He could have sworn he heard birdsong. He closed his eyes and leaned towards Opal. Just as their lips were about to meet, Bertram saw stars...

...which, as he realised a split second later, were caused by something very large and hard hitting him on the back of the head.

Chapter Three

How Bertram put Opal's Back up, and discovered that Troll sports just Aren't Cricket.

"Ouch!" The large, hard thing fell to the ground. It was a rock.

Rubbing his head, Bertram turned round to see where it had come from – and groaned. Granite Moraine! That was all he needed!

Granite was bottom of every class at Doctor Chalk's Academy and top at every sport. Most troll games required strength and brutality rather than skill, and mindless violence was Granite's speciality. He was ugly, stupid and brutal – even by troll standards. His nose looked as if someone had used heavy mining equipment on it. His eyes were small and piggy, rimmed with red. He had a jaw capable of cracking rocks, which was just as well, as that was generally what he used it for. Talking was an effort for Granite – at least, talking in sentences. He mostly talked in threats and preferred using words no longer than "Duh!"

Granite's muscles were impressive, to trolls who were impressed by that sort of thing (including Beryl, Garnet and Topaz, who thought Granite was "hunky"). He *worked in*, which was like working out, except it used less space and consisted of squeezing things until they became smaller things. Granite liked to throw his arms round a lump of sedimentary rock as large as himself and hug it until it crumbled into gravel.

He had been known to do the same sort of thing to other trolls.

Granite picked up the rock he had thrown at Bertram and tossed it around casually – bicep to hand, bicep to hand. Then he spun the rock on one finger. It made a screeching noise and wisps of smoke drifted up from the bottom where friction against Granite's finger heated it to melting point. His mean little eyes, squinting out from their scaly lids like small, cowardly scavengers peeping from their caves, took in the bench... Opal... Bertram and his pathetic gift.

Opal gave Granite an unfriendly look. "Oh, fossils, not you!"

Granite threw the rock again. It bounced off Bertram's forehead. "You wanna play trolleyball?"

Bertram enjoyed trolleyball. It was the only troll sport he was any good at. Because Bertram was light on his feet (for a troll) he was particularly adept at jumping to smash the ball over the net (the move called a 'spike'). But he didn't want to play a game now – especially the way Granite probably played it. "No thanks."

Granite leered mockingly at him. "Wassa matter? You scared? Scared to play wiv the big trolls?" He threw the rock ball again.

Bertram angrily batted it aside. It smashed the tip off a stalactite and rolled away. "I told you, Granite – not now."

"That's cuz you're no good at it."

"If you like," Bertram said indifferently. He turned his back on Granite.

A heavily-muscled arm landed across Bertram's shoulders with the force of an avalanche. A voice in his ear, accompanied by breath that smelt like mine-gas, grated, "Go an' get the ball."

Bertram looked at the rock-ball, which was lying in a shallow puddle beside the path. "Why me?"

"Cuz you dropped it. You drop it, you gotta go get it."

"You threw it at me."

"You arguin'?"

"Oh, for rock's sake!" Opal stamped her foot, leaving a small crater in the paving. She stood up, flounced across to the ball and handed it over to Granite. "Here's your ball, tough guy. Now go away."

Granite glowered at Bertram through piggy eyes, clenching and unclenching his ham-like fists. He turned to Opal. "Is this troll botherin' you?"

Unimpressed, Opal put her hands on her hips. "No."

"Cuz if he was, I could squeeze him for you, no problem."

"Granite, you are so dense. I told you, he's not bothering me."

"If you say so." Without looking at Bertram, Granite gave him a shove that propelled him into an iron glow-post, which buckled. He struck a he-troll pose. "Howz about you come wiv me. I can show you a good time, trollop. You wanna go to *The Cavern*?"

Opal shook her head angrily. "I've told you before, Granite, all this cave-troll stuff doesn't cut any marble with me. Anyway, Bertram has already asked me to go to *The Rocksie*."

"Um..." Bertram blinked at this piece of fiction. He hadn't done any such thing! He didn't like nightclubs. When trolls came out at night and started waving clubs about, someone was going to get hurt, and Bertram had no illusions about who that "someone" was likely to be. In any case, he'd told his mother he'd be back early.

Granite pounced on his hesitation. "See? Baby's scared to go to da club. Whadda loser!" He laughed with a sound like rocks tumbling down a shaft.

Opal turned her glare on Bertram. "Bertram? Are you coming or not?"

"Well... I..." Bertram mumbled unhappily.

"Oh, I give up!" Opal snorted. "Suit yourself." She tossed her head angrily and stomped off. Flakes of rock fell from the cave ceiling.

Bertram called after her, "I'll meet you tomorrow – on the way to school..."

Opal wheeled round. "Don't bother. I know the way – and if I feel the need for protection, I'm sure I can find a picksie who'll do a better job than you!" She marched on down the path and out of sight. Bertram groaned.

A giant hand spun Bertram round. He found himself nose-to-nose with Granite, whose eyes were narrowed to slits. In a voice like the grinding of ice over rock, the bigger troll said, "Lissen, you. Stay away from my trollop."

Bertram glared at Granite. His mother was right. "Trollop" wasn't a polite word for a female troll, especially one like Opal. And it sounded particularly unpleasant when a troll like Granite used it.

Amazing himself by his own daring, Bertram said, "She's not your girl."

Granite flexed his muscles. "Yeah?"

"Yeah!" said Bertram.

"Yeah?"

"Yeah!" Bertram felt he was getting the hang of this conversation.

Granite stepped back, never taking his eyes off Bertram's. He stuck two fingers like bollards into his cavern of a mouth and blew. A piercing whistle echoed around the cave.

At the summons, two more trolls glided into view. Bertram realised that they were on troller skates – and that he was in big trouble.

It was generally thought at Doctor Chalk's Academy that Granite kept Gabbro and Wolframite around for three reasons. The first was that they were so stupid they made Granite himself look halfway intelligent by comparison. If there was a battle of wits between Gabbro, Wolframite and a small piece of flint, the flint would probably win, even if the other two cheated. The second reason was that they were completely indifferent to pain – their own, or other people's. And thirdly, they always did what Granite told them.

Both Gabbro and Wolframite were wearing hockey uniforms and unpleasant grins. They each carried two curved iron clubs.

Granite clicked his fingers. Wolframite passed him a pair of heavy iron skates which he strapped on. He signalled again and two clubs were thrust into his hands. He gripped one and slammed the other into Bertram's chest. "Can you play troller hockey?"

Bertram, with his arms wrapped round the club, gasped for breath. Troller hockey was a really violent sport. He shook his head.

"You're gonna learn."

"But I haven't got any skates," Bertram protested.

"Good." Granite stood up and poked Bertram in the chest with the end of his club. "You're in goal."

Granite and his hench-trolls swooped, and Bertram found himself the target of a nightmare attack. His tormentors skated too fast for Bertram to follow, much less dodge. Sometimes they used their clubs to hit rocks at him, blasting them with such force that he could hear the air being torn apart, and those that missed him would shatter explosively against the walls of the cavern. Next moment, Granite and his thugs would slam into Bertram, sending him spinning to the floor. Sometimes they hooked their clubs around his feet, hauling his legs from beneath him.

When Bertram was too bruised and winded to stand, Granite signalled to the others to stop. He swooped in and held his hockey club across Bertram's throat, almost choking him.

"I don't like you," said Granite conversationally.

Bertram coughed. "I'd noticed," he wheezed.

"I don't like you," Granite went on, "'cuz you hang around my trollop. An' I don't like you cuz you're littler than me. An' I don't like you cuz you're no good at troller hockey. An' I don't like you cuz your mum's weird an' so are you. You're not a proper troll – you're just a... a *thing*!"

Bertram managed to gasp, "Leave my mum out of this," but Granite wasn't listening.

"An' I don't like you," he continued, "cuz you do stupid cooking. An' I don't like you cuz you go outside an' talk about the sun like it was sumthin' good, an' go on all about the little lovely fluffy animals and birds singin' an' grass an' fings. What's that got to do with trolls? Eh? We don't need that stuff. What's it got to do with *us*?"

Bertram stared at his assailant in astonishment. He'd never before heard the brutish troll say so many words all at once. By Granite's standards, this was eloquence.

"You lissen," said Granite, "and you lissen good. I'm gonna hurt you. And then I'm gonna hurt you some more. I'm gonna hurt you most if I see you with Opal again, but even if I don't, I'm gonna hurt you anyway. Wherever you go, whatever you do, whoever you're with, I'm gonna hurt you. You can't stop me. Nobody's gonna help you because everybody knows you're a strange, weird troll who's not like them."

Granite unstrapped his skates and stood up. "What shall we play next?" he asked cheerfully, as Bertram wheezed and clutched at his throat. "We played trolleyball, an' we played troller hockey. I know, how about roxing?"

Bertram, still on his hands and knees, looked up. "Bare knuckle?" he suggested hopefully.

Granite picked up a rock in each fist and leered at him. "Nah."

Both Bertram's arms were grabbed from behind. He gave a gasp of shock and struggled wildly, twisting his head from side to side. Wolframite was holding his left arm, Gabbro his right. Their grip was unbreakable. The two trolls stamped their feet rhythmically and began to sing, in their rumbling voices, an ancient war chant of the trolls...

"We are gonna rock you!
We are gonna rock you!"

Bertram was turned to face Granite who advanced inexorably, eyes gleaming, mouth stretched into a hideous grin, clicking the rocks in his hands together with every step. There was no escape. Granite meant business.

Bertram was caught between a rock and a hard place.

Chapter Four

How Bertram was Saved from a Pounding, and Councillor Shale began his Tale.

"In the name of all that's subterranean, what is going on here?"

Granite's hench-trolls stopped chanting and let go of Bertram's arms as if they'd suddenly become white-hot.

Bertram turned. The voice belonged to Councillor Shale, one of the most important trolls in the city and a leading member of the Trollmoot, the council of Caer Borundum. He was also, of course, Opal's uncle.

From the tip of his snow-white crest to the shiny toes of his bat-skin boots, Councillor Shale was every inch a gentle-troll. His imposing bearing and rich, powerful voice had succeeded in quelling many unruly meetings of the Trollmoot. It certainly had a quelling effect on Granite Moraine and his thugs. They wilted into pathetic, cringing yes-trolls in the blink of an eye.

Councillor Shale nailed Granite with a look that would have bored a hole clean through a diamond. "Moraine, isn't it? What do you think you're up to?"

Granite looked down and shuffled his feet. "Nuthin', Couns'lor Shale, sir."

"Really?"

Granite squirmed. "We wuz just playin'," he rumbled sulkily.

"Playin'!" echoed Gabbro and Wolframite, nodding their heads in desperate agreement.

Councillor Shale rubbed the side of his nose with his gold-topped cane. "Indeed?" he said coldly. "I should have thought that three young trolls of your age and undoubted gifts..." (Gabbro and Wolframite went cross-eyed trying to imagine what 'gifts' the councillor had in mind) "...would be able to find more profitable ways of spending your time." Councillor Shale gazed at each troll in turn. "Ways that would involve your being *somewhere else*."

Granite gave a nervous nod. He cuffed his stooges on the side of the head and dragged them forcefully away.

Councillor Shale watched them out of sight. Then he walked ponderously to a bench, dusted it with a spider-silk pocket handkerchief and sat down. He gave Bertram a look of sorrowful benevolence.

"Oh, Bertram, Bertram," he said. "What are we going to do with you?"

Bertram guessed that this was a question to which no answer was expected, so he didn't give one.

Councillor Shale sighed. "What was that all about? My niece, I suppose."

"That's what started it – me being with Opal. But even if I hadn't been, Granite would still have picked a fight." Bertram shrugged. "He just doesn't like me."

Councillor Shale gave him a shrewd look. "And that worries you?"

"Well, yes," said Bertram. "Granite can make life pretty tough. But he's stupid. I don't want him bullying me, but I don't care what he *thinks*. Other trolls bother me more."

"How so?"

"I mean, a bully like Granite can always find some excuse to get me. The trolls who upset me are the ones who are normal and decent and say 'hello' when they meet each other in the tunnels, even if they don't know each other very well. Except when they see me, they don't say 'hello', they just look away and hurry past as if I'm invisible or something..." Bertram stopped in confusion. "Am I making any sense at all?"

"You are pellucidity itself."

Bertram stared at Councillor Shale. "Pardon?"

"I mean, I know exactly what you mean." The older troll reverted to silence, apparently lost in thought.

Shale was an old family friend. Bertram had often been to his house in Silver Street, one of the most exclusive areas of Caer Borundum. It was there that he had met Opal. The councillor had always been very kind to Bertram and his mother, sending them gifts of food when times were hard. He was probably the only troll that Bertram could talk to without feeling embarrassed. Many times, he had listened to Bertram's descriptions of the creatures that lived in the world outside, or discussed stargazing or cookery. Councillor Shale never seemed surprised or worried by Bertram's 'un-trollish' interests. Bertram sometimes felt that Councillor Shale, wise and kindly, was the only troll who really understood him.

Abruptly, the older troll stood up. "Come along. It's time you and I had a proper talk." Obediently, Bertram fell into step alongside the councillor, who set off at a measured pace, out of the park and into the city.

At first they walked through the suburbs of Caer Borundum, where troll dwellings or 'delves' were small and set apart, protected from the world and each other by painstakingly maintained barriers of stalactites and stalagmites. These delves had names like *Duntrollin* and *Clay Nous*. Some of the delves had been made by volcanic action (a sign above one door read: *Two Lavas Built This Nest*); others had been hand-hewn by generations of trolls, who had simply dug an extra room or two as their families grew bigger.

As they approached the centre of Caer Borundum, the pace of life increased. There were more glow-globes, and more traffic on the streets. Cabs and carriages pulled by high-stepping elf-ants – insects that stood as high as an adult troll's shoulder – jostled for space in the crowded tunnels, their drivers cracking their whips as the elf-ants waved their feelers threateningly at each other. The rumble of wheels echoed around the stone walls.

Their route led them through the larger caverns of the business district, where glow-globes shone from the windows of high-rock developments carved into every cave-wall and carrier-bats flitted from office to office, chittering urgently. They passed the Dreary Lane Theatre, which was showing the famous troll tragedy, *'Tis Pity She's An Ore.* On either side of the road were shops displaying rare stone, clothing and ironware, and stalls and restaurants selling food. Traders who recognised the councillor were calling out to attract his attention to their wares.

"How are you, Councillor Shale? I've got some lovely plump bats just in, nice and juicy..."

"Cave fungus, Councillor? Handpicked today..."

"Special offer on grit today, Councillor – half-price, fresh from the mill..."

To these offers (and others: of best end of mole, newly caught rock salmon and toad in the hole) the councillor responded with a wave of his hand and a shake of his head. He threaded his way between the tables of pavement cafés, where well-dressed trolls were relaxing over drinks of coal-a-cola (with gneiss and a slice of limestone) or mineral water on the rocks. Bertram followed, trying to ignore the fact that the café patrons, though they greeted the councillor, looked straight through Bertram as though he wasn't there at all.

Soon afterwards, vibration of the ground beneath his feet told Bertram that they were nearing the river. Together, they crossed the troll-bridge through air filled with spume from the roaring, gushing water that swept by below, racing headlong downstream towards the terrible Trollenbach Falls.

Finally, they arrived at the councillor's imposing town-delve. Shale took a key from his coat pocket and opened the great iron door. Bertram followed him inside, glancing round at the familiar room with its carved stone furniture, spider-silk hangings and cave paintings of important trolls, all long-dead.

Councillor Shale's delve was grand, but typical of troll houses. The large central chamber where Bertram now stood served as the living and dining room. Passageways led off into more rooms – a kitchen, bedrooms, storerooms, a bathroom and Councillor Shale's study. It was to this room, comfortably furnished with deep marble armchairs and pumice cushions, that the councillor led his guest. He gestured to one of the armchairs, then crossed to his great stone desk where he sat, his chin resting on his hands, gazing at Bertram who fidgeted uncomfortably.

At that moment, the study door opened and Opal walked in. "Uncle..." she began, but broke off as Bertram stood up politely. "Oh."

The councillor smiled warmly at his niece. "What is it, my dear?"

"Well..." Opal shot Bertram another dubious glance.

Councillor Shale's eyes twinkled satirically. "Don't tell me you lovebirds have fallen out?"

Opal's eyes widened. "Lovebirds? Let me tell you..." Catching her uncle's look, she drew herself up haughtily.

"You're making fun of me. You know perfectly well that Bertram and I are the merest acquaintances." She glared at Bertram, who wriggled again. "Scarcely that even, if he can't be bothered to take a girl out once in a while." She tossed her head. "What's he doing here anyway?"

"I found him about to be beaten to a sediment by Granite Moraine and his sidekicks. I thought he'd be safer here with us." The councillor looked at Opal's angry face and gave an amused chuckle. "Perhaps I was wrong." His tone became more serious. "You shouldn't have left him alone, you know."

Opal stuck her nose in the air. "I'm sure I don't see how a feeble girl like me could possibly protect a big, strong he-troll like Bertram..."

"That's not fair!" Bertram protested. "There were three of them. I didn't stand a chance..."

Opal sniffed. "Well, you shouldn't have annoyed them."

"*Annoyed* them...?" Bertram was thunderstruck.

Councillor Shale shook his head. "Ignore her, Bertram. She's only trying to make you lose your temper. Her mother used to do that to me all the time." Opal snorted. "What was it you wanted, my dear?"

"Mister Stibnite called from the mine. He said there was a problem with Number Eight shaft – lava flows in the lower levels. He said he thought it might be the salamanders again."

Councillor Shale owned Igneous Conglomerates, the biggest mining company in Caer Borundum. His mines provided the city with limestone, iron ore and coal, precious stones such as diamond, ruby and emerald, and valuable metals – gold and silver.

The councillor shook his head in annoyance. "Stibnite's a terrible old fusspot. We were going to close Number Eight anyway – it's practically worked out. Just tell him to put a temporary cap on it. We'll send a roughneck team down tomorrow to find out exactly what the problem is."

"Yes, Uncle." Opal gave Bertram a final withering glance and stalked out. From an adjoining room, Bertram heard a succession of taps as she beat out the message on a large stalactite growing from the ceiling. A vein of conductive rock would carry the vibrations of the tapped code to the mine, where Mr Stibnite would no doubt be anxiously awaiting his employer's instructions. Few families owned a trollegraph line, but it was quicker than using carrier-bats – and more reliable, since the bats sometimes went missing (believed eaten).

Councillor Shale steepled his thick fingers and mused. "These deep mining operations are proving to be difficult," he said. "The higher levels are increasingly worked out – or the veins run across our borders into the country of the gnomes. We've asked them to sell us the mineral rights, but I'm sure you can guess their answer."

Bertram grinned. "Gno?"

Shale gave a bark of laughter. "Hah! Exactly. But the deep shafts take us ever closer to the realm of the salamanders, and the fire-lizards are beginning to show their displeasure by flooding the lower workings with lava. Trolls may be resistant to high temperatures, but I can't ask my men to go swimming in molten rock!" He shook himself. "I'm sorry, Bertram – you don't want to hear about my troubles, when you have enough of your own. Why don't you tell me about them?" He nodded towards the closed door, behind which Opal's tapping could still be heard. "Starting with my niece."

Bertram shrugged helplessly. "I can't really blame her for being angry. She's a normal troll. I'm not. She wants to do the sort of things normal trolls do. I'm not interested in that stuff. Like today. I couldn't take her to *The Rocksie* because I told my mum I'd be there when she got home. You know how she worries." The councillor nodded sympathetically. "Opal did try to get rid of Granite and I let her down, I suppose."

The councillor pursed his lips. "Have you tried to get her involved in the things that interest you?"

"How?" Bertram shook his head. "She can do cookery, but she doesn't like it much. To show her the other things, I'd have to take her outside... and I can't do that."

"No," said the councillor grimly. "Because of the Man-curse."

Bertram stared at him. "The Man-curse?"

Councillor Shale continued as if he had not heard Bertram's question: "You know you are different. You know you are not the same as other trolls." Bertram stared into the councillor's solemn face and nodded mutely. He could not have spoken to save his life.

"It is time you learnt why."

Chapter Five

Of Desperate Battles, Dreadful Weapons and Dirty Deeds.

"I have a tale to recount to you," said the old troll. "A story that goes back through the ages to the very twilight of our history."

Bertram stared at Councillor Shale in bewilderment. He'd thought he was going to find out why he was different, not have a history lesson!

"There is much to learn from our past, Bertram. Perhaps in the foundations of our past, we may make out the shape of our future."

Bertram nodded, though he hadn't a clue where this was leading.

"The history of the trolls, Bertram," Councillor Shale continued, "is a history of great deeds, betrayal and tyranny."

"Oh, is it?" Bertram tried to sound enthusiastic.

The councillor gave Bertram a searching stare. "What do you know of the human race?"

"Not much," Bertram replied truthfully. On his many trips to the outside world, he had never once met a human. He'd only seen pictures of them on the slates his mother brought home from the library.

"Let me tell you about humans." The old troll's voice was grave. "They are the opposite of our race in many ways. We are creatures of the dark. They are creatures of the light. Sunlight gives humans life, but for trolls it means death." Councillor Shale rested his chin on his hands and gazed at Bertram intently. "Did you know that we trolls were once rulers of the outside world?" He paused to allow Bertram a moment to realise the significance of his statement.

"You mean that trolls used to go out? In the sun?"

The older troll nodded. "Yes."

Bertram was amazed. Doctor Chalk had never mentioned this in his lessons. "But sunlight turns trolls into stone!"

"Yes – all trolls, except you." Once again, Councillor Shale paused, as if expecting Bertram to say something. Once again, Bertram could think of nothing to say.

The councillor sighed heavily. "Did you think that being turned to stone by the sun was something we inherited from our ancestors? Something fundamental to our species, like having four fingers on each hand?" Councillor Shale shook his head. "No, my boy. The light of day is death to trolls for quite another reason.

"Back in the dawn of history, the trolls were masters of all known lands: mountains, moors and Forest. The peoples of the underground world and the world above were ruled by a succession of great troll kings."

Rising abruptly, Councillor Shale strode to an enormous slate-case that stood against the wall and took down an ancient-looking silver box which was decorated with small gemstones. The old troll held the box almost reverentially and read out the intricate engraving on its lid:

An Account of the Troll Kings of the Stygian Era and Beyond.
As written by the esteemed and venerable bard,
Jasper Rubble Rock Trollkein.

Councillor Shale's eyes glinted. "They're all here, Bertram. The Glorious Stygian Kings." He opened up the box, unfolded a moleskin dust cloth and began to pull out a number of slates. "Tartarus the Murky; Iron the Terrible; Igneous the Hot; Boron the Hard; Gravel the Crunchy. All great and powerful warriors, Bertram. They ruled the known worlds of light and dark for hundreds of years from their seat of power, the Obsidian Throne in the great palace of Trollingrad, the capital city of all trolldom." Councillor Shale placed the slates on his marble table. He knew by heart the story he was to relate. His eyes darkened and he continued his tale...

"Then, one sad day, the humans came: small bands of

explorers from lands far away. These explorers were followed by traders, hoping to make their fortunes. Treaties were agreed. At first our races lived together in peace. The humans accepted the trolls as their rightful rulers. Troll and human prospered.

"But the humans were greedy. They demanded more and more land: and when we refused it, they attacked us. And so the Troll-Man Wars began. Of course, the humans were no match for our mighty armies and we easily defeated them."

Councillor Shale closed his eyes and his brow furrowed. "But then came the sorcerers: wizards, mages, spellbinders, enchanters." Councillor Shale spat out each word. "Evil men, with the power to shape magic and bend it to their will. These creatures of the demonic arts combined their wicked powers to place a terrible curse on the troll race – the Man-curse."

Bertram gaped, spellbound. "The Man-curse?"

"From that day on, any troll who ventured into the outside world and was caught in the rays of the sun would be turned to stone forever:

'One sun to slay them all
One sun to blind them
One sun to stone them all
And with its brightness bind them...'

"The humans chose their time well. The mighty troll army under the command of King Boron the Hard had gathered at a small river town known as Troll Harbour to inflict a final crushing defeat on the humans. But at high noon, mages appeared on the hills above the town. Hastily, the troll generals formed ranks and marched to the battle, little knowing that the sorcerers had planned a cowardly sneak attack. As the mages chanted their evil incantations, the clouds rolled away and the sun shone with a brightness no troll had ever seen before.

"Then the sorcerers waved their hands, making signs of dreadful power over our magnificent, invincible army – and lo! The front ranks stopped still – and never moved again. They had been turned to stone where they stood.

"The contagion spread. Rank after rank of trolls was turned into stone. The sunlight caused their blood to solidify, their veins to harden and their arteries to clog as the curse took effect. Soon the cries of the stricken were silenced as their lungs congealed in their bodies and their heads fossilised. King Boron and his army were no more.

"The humans rejoiced. They tore down the great palace of Trollingrad, raising their own city on the site in pride and defiance of their enemies."

Bertram was spellbound. "Didn't any of the trolls survive?"

The councillor shook his head sorrowfully. "A few. A pitiful few. They sought a final refuge, travelling at night and sheltering during the day in the shadows of the Dark Forest."

"The Dark Forest!" The name filled Bertram with a mixture of excitement and dread.

"The survivors gathered in the ancient underground

strongholds of our people. Desperately, they sought something to counter the Man-curse, some weapon that would allow us to stride once again into the outside world and reclaim that which was taken from us by trickery and spiteful malice."

Councillor Shale removed two more slates from the silver box and held them out for Bertram's inspection. On one was the image of a ball of gold encrusted with gemstones. On the other was the picture of a solid gold rod, with a large crystal (a diamond? wondered Bertram) mounted at the tip. It, too, was covered in gemstones. Even Bertram, with his limited knowledge of rocks and minerals, felt awed by the exquisite artistry revealed by the etchings.

"The Orb and the Sceptre of the Last Stygian Kings," explained the older troll. "The final symbols of troll majesty."

"They're beautiful," breathed Bertram.

"Beautiful and powerful," agreed Councillor Shale. "For they were mighty instruments. The Sceptre was a weapon for the battlefield. It cast a shadow over the troll host so that it could attack the humans even during the hours of daylight. But the Orb was a weapon of last resort. It was made to darken the skies of the entire world, so that men should freeze and die in the darkness.

"Preparations were made. A secret stronghold was dug. The Hall of the Mountain King was the final refuge of the trolls. There the Obsidian Throne, rescued from the wreck of Trollingrad, was set. There, King Gravel, the last of the Troll Kings, gathered together the last army of the trolls.

"But before the Orb and Sceptre could be used, the humans struck. Whether they found out our refuge by luck or guile, or whether we were betrayed, I do not know. But they attacked before our weapons were ready.

"Battle was joined, but without the powers of the Orb and Sceptre, the struggle was futile. The troll cavalry on their magnificent war-moles made one last desperate charge with King Gravel at their head – but it was hopeless. They were cut down in their hundreds. The Charge of the Troll Brigade was the final act of the Troll-Man Wars. We were defeated." The old troll hung his head and sighed.

"Of the defenders, not one survived. The defeat was so total that the Hall of the Mountain King, the Orb, the Sceptre and the Obsidian Throne were lost. The last treasures of trollkind passed out of all knowledge of the scattered remnants that stumbled to hide, miserable and defeated, in the dark underground places of the world.

"The time that followed is known as the Dark Ages. Over many years, the few survivors of trollkind made their way to the caverns beneath this remote mountain and began to build Caer Borundum." The councillor's voice was weary. "Some think this place was chosen because it was the scene of our last stand against humanity, and that the Hall of the Mountain King still lies hidden somewhere in the depths of our realm, waiting to be rediscovered." The old troll spread his hands in a gesture of helplessness. "Who knows?"

"Don't the slates say?" asked Bertram.

Councillor Shale shook his head. "They are the only

records we have of those days and they are incomplete." He looked Bertram in the eye. "They were discovered in the library, by your mother. She brought them to me."

"She never told me any of this," said Bertram.

"There are other things she has not told you, Bertram." The councillor rose from his desk and stood before Bertram. Suddenly, he didn't look like a safe and comfortable old troll any more. With his hands clasped behind his back, under the tails of his coat, and his eyes glinting as they reflected the phosphorescent radiance of the glow-globe, he looked stern and a little frightening, but his voice remained soft. "You are different from other trolls for one very good reason. You are not exactly a troll."

Bertram stared in bewilderment. A dozen different feelings coursed through his body. Anxiety, puzzlement, horror – relief. The answer to why he was different was in his grasp, but did he want to know? "What do you mean, 'not exactly a troll'?" he asked. "What am I?"

The councillor ignored Bertram's question. "Many years ago, a strange troll arrived at the gates of our city."

"A strange troll?" Bertram was mystified. "But I thought there weren't any trolls outside Caer Borundum."

"So did we all. The stranger was brought before the Trollmoot. He said his name was Malachite and claimed to be the last survivor of a troll colony in the far north. He said that he had travelled by night for many months to reach us. The Trollmoot appointed me to investigate his claims. I enlisted your mother to search the records for the stranger's missing colony. I encouraged her to question the stranger." The old troll hung his head. "I could not have foreseen that she would fall in love with him."

Bertram stared at Councillor Shale with mounting horror.

"Then suddenly the stranger disappeared – leaving a note from which your mother and I learnt the dreadful truth. There was no lost colony. The 'stranger' was not a troll at all. He was a human in disguise. An enchanter. He had come to spy on us. When he had learnt all he could, he left. And shortly afterwards, you were born." Councillor Shale broke off and looked steadily at Bertram.

An ice-cold hand seemed to clutch at Bertram's heart. "Are you saying that this stranger... was my father?"

The councillor nodded. "I felt responsible. I took a special interest in your mother, and in you, Bertram. I tried to persuade Pumice to tell you the truth, but..." The old troll gave a heavy sigh. "I suppose she was too ashamed. At all events, now you know."

Bertram couldn't speak. Deep sobs welled in his chest and he fought to keep back the tears.

"That is why you can venture into the outside world, Bertram. That is why the Man-curse doesn't affect you. That is why you have human qualities."

Bertram closed his eyes and tried not to listen to what he knew was about to be said.

Councillor Shale's voice was compassionate but inexorable. "You are half-troll – half-human!"

Chapter Six

How Bertram the Half-troll considered Half-measures until a Gossip gave him a Piece of her Mind.

Bertram wandered through the shadowy tunnels of Caer Borundum in a daze.

He had rushed from Councillor Shale's house in a state of such panic and horror that he had not even heard the old troll's cries of "Bertram! Wait!" He had simply needed to get away.

But now Bertram hardly knew where he was or where he was going. Twice he stepped off the pavement into the roadway, causing trolleybuses and delivery carts to swerve. Bertram walked on, oblivious to the angry shouts of the drivers, the complaints of the passengers and the unhappy grunting of the moles.

At length, he found himself beside the Troll River without any idea how he'd arrived there. As he leant against the parapet and gazed at the dark, rushing waters, Bertram's confused mind began to settle and some of his jumbled thoughts started to make sense.

He wasn't 'exactly' a troll – well, that explained a lot! It explained why he could go out in daylight without turning to stone, why he was so attracted to the outside world and why he disliked the dark. That was his human inheritance. It also explained why he felt so uncomfortable around other trolls, and why they felt he was weird. Now Bertram understood the reason his mother had never liked talking about his father and why she always seemed so quiet and sad. His eyes filled with oily tears. Had she been happy when her half-troll son was born, or horrified? Did *she* think he was a monster? Maybe Granite was right, maybe he was just a *thing*.

And what was he to do now? Should he pretend that none of this mattered? Should he finish school and go to work at the mills that pulverised the rock from Councillor Shale's mines ("the daily grind", as it was known)? Or maybe he should get an office job, shuffling stacks of slate. Bertram shook his head. He'd never felt he belonged in Caer Borundum and now he knew it for a fact. Yet where else was there to go?

Well... he was half-human. If the trolls didn't want him, could he live with humans? Even in his misery, Bertram almost laughed out loud at the absurdity of the idea. Despite the human side of his heritage, he still looked like a troll.

Bertram couldn't see humans getting along with a huge, grey, scaly-skinned creature who dressed in moleskins, ate powdered rock and also happened to be a deadly enemy. In any case, he had no idea where humans lived.

He had to talk to someone – but who? Not Opal – he couldn't face her now that he knew the truth. The same applied to the few classmates at school Bertram thought of as friends – well, friendly – or at least, not hostile... How could he share this terrible secret with them? No, there was only one person in Bertram's world he could talk to about this: his mother.

He turned away from the river and, with dragging steps, set off to find her.

So late in the day, the library was almost empty. The entrance-cavern was quiet. An old troll with a news-slate on his lap snored quietly in a chair. The only other sign of life was Gossip Adamant, the old picksie who cleaned the library. She was busily sweeping the already immaculately dust-free stone floor with a molehair broom.

She looked up as Bertram approached. "Oh, 'ello, Master Bertram. You come to see your mother?" Bertram nodded. "You're a good boy. Young trolls today, I don't know what the underworld's coming to. No respect for us old-uns. Not that I'm complaining. Nobody can say I'm the complaining sort. Live and let live, that's my motto. Still, a few pleases and thank yous wouldn't go amiss, that's all I'm saying." She gave an enormous sniff. Then she looked round and dropped her voice to a conspiratorial whisper. "Listen, now you're here, you couldn't do me a favour could you?"

"What sort of favour?" asked Bertram guardedly.

"There's a bit of encrustation over there." Gossip Adamant pointed to a wall of the cavern where a drip had allowed a collection of mineral crystals to form an unsightly blotch against the smooth stone. "I know it's a job for the Works Department, really, but I've been asking for something to be done about it for ever so long and nobody listens."

Bertram looked down at the old picksie in dismay. "I don't know that I should..."

"Oh, go on!" Gossip Adamant gave him a wink and tapped the side of her nose. It made a pinging sound. "There's nobody to see."

Bertram sighed. "Oh, all right."

He waited, looking around nervously, while Gossip Adamant tucked her skirt up tight. Then Bertram grasped her firmly by the ankles – and swung her hard, so that her beaky nose slammed into the discoloured patch, chipping the crystals away from the rock.

Gossip Adamant twisted her head and gave Bertram a disgusted look. "Come on, young man! You've barely scratched it. You'll have to do better than that!"

"Sorry." Gritting his teeth, Bertram swung again. Crystals flew.

"Harder!"

With Bertram swinging with all his might, Gossip Adamant's iron-hard nose shattered the remaining crystals. The sound echoed round the cavern. The old troll with the news-slate snorted in his sleep and wriggled in his chair.

When the crystals had all been chipped away, Bertram put the old picksie down. She inspected the rock closely. She rubbed the dust from the tip of her nose with a handkerchief and blew into it with a noise like a trolleybus horn. Then she smiled at Bertram.

"There now!" she said breezily. "That's better. Worryin' me somethin' dreadful, that was." She untucked her skirts and bent down to pick up her broom.

Bertram said, "Do you *like* doing that?"

Gossip Adamant straightened up again, and stared at him in bafflement. As far as she was concerned, Bertram might as well have asked, "Do you *like* breathing?"

"I mean," Bertram persisted, "doesn't it hurt?"

The old picksie stroked her long, hard, pointed nose and chuckled. "Bless you, no. Why for would it? Us picksies have been chippin' away at that old rock for hundreds of years. We'm used to it."

"But is it what you always wanted to do?" Bertram gazed at Gossip Adamant's uncomprehending face, trying desperately to find the words that would make her understand. "I mean, when you were young, did you look forward to the day when a troll-miner would choose you for his pick, and take you down the mine to spend the next forty years chipping at stone with your nose?"

Gossip Adamant sighed happily. "Forty-three year I were

down that pit. Never missed a day. Not even when I were expectin' our little Silicon. I had her in me lunch break."

Bertram clenched his fists in frustration. "But was that the life you *really* wanted?"

The old picksie stared at Bertram as if he were mad. "What else would I go fer to do?" she demanded. "Mining's what my father did. And my mother. And their fathers before them. And their mothers. And their grandfathers before them. And their grandmothers. And their great—"

"Yes, yes, I know that," Bertram interrupted. "But didn't you ever want to do something else?"

Gossip Adamant simply gawped at him.

"I do," said Bertram savagely, suddenly knowing that it was true. "I don't want to live down here under the mountain where it's always dark. I don't want to be a miner, or a fungus-farmer, or a bat-catcher. I don't want to be a troll."

"That's wicked talk, that is!" Gossip Adamant flapped at Bertram with her apron. "Shame on you! We are what we was made, an' there's no point complainin' or tryin' to be what we're not. I never heard of such a thing!" She glared and wagged her nose. "I've seen this comin', mark you. I told your mother a hundred times, 'Pumice, you must be harder on the boy' – but did she listen? No! I don't know, I really don't..."

Bertram wished he'd kept his thoughts to himself. Picksies lived in tiny delves in the part of town where nobody else wanted to live, and worked down the mines for very little reward. When their noses became too soft for mining, they usually became cleaners or watchmen. They never complained, no matter how hard their lives were.

"You just think on, Master Bertram!" Gossip Adamant fixed him with a steely glare. "The ways of providence is deep an' dark, and we all has our parts to play. There ain't no point in bats wishin' they was moles an' moles' wishin' they was bats. Bats can't dig an' moles can't fly, an' decent folk stays where they're put!" With that, the old picksie shouldered her broom and stamped out of the library, slamming the door behind her. The old troll woke up with a start, put his news-slate back on the rack and shuffled off.

As Bertram headed towards the stairs leading to his mother's office, Gossip Adamant's words echoed in his mind: "Decent folks stays where they're put". But Bertram's heritage put him nowhere. He wanted to talk to his mother – nothing she could say would alter the facts: Bertram was neither a proper troll, nor a proper human.

Suddenly changing his mind, Bertram instead walked out of the library. He turned back once. One window of the library was lit – the window on the second floor where, though he couldn't see her, Bertram knew his mother would be peering at the faint scratches of writing on a worn-out slate and transferring the ancient words to a fresh one. So that the history of the trolls should not be lost. So that, with her mind full of the legends of her people, she should never have to think too hard about her own story or the son who was the result of it.

Bertram felt ashamed. Ashamed of his mother, for keeping his ancestry a secret; ashamed of not being a troll; and ashamed of being part human – a race that could inflict such a thing as a Man-curse on other peoples.

He turned away and wandered out into the deserted tunnels, alone.

Chapter Seven

How Bertram went Over, Down, Under and Out.

How long Bertram walked, he couldn't say, but eventually he found himself on the track that followed the course of the Troll River as it gouged its way through the rocky caverns on the outskirts of Caer Borundum.

A distant roar grew louder and louder as Bertram plodded along a gravel pathway that eventually led into a large cavern. Veins of blue crystal lined its walls, casting a soft, luminous glow upon the naked rock.

When the roar became so deafening that it could no longer be ignored, Bertram glanced up and realised he had arrived at the Trollenbach Falls. Here, the river spilled over a sheer cliff face, hurtling down into the gaping chasm below. The pounding from the falls was almost mind-numbing as it reverberated round the cavern. The rock walls shook from the force of the mighty deluge.

Bertram leaned over the ropes and iron railings that stretched along the edge of the track to prevent any troll falling into the foaming water and being swept over the falls to certain death. This was the scene of many a foolhardy escapade and tragedy. Several trolls had tried to swim across the river just above the falls. The strong current had made short work of them. Even the great illusionist, Trollini, had failed in his attempt to beat the falls. He'd been nailed into a barrel and thrown into the river – never to be seen again, although several pieces of barrel were later recovered. They now formed part of an exhibit on *Really Stupid And Pointless Ways To Kill Yourself* in Caer Borundum's Museum.

Where the river narrowed, two rocks protruded either side of the falls. This spot was known as Lovers' Plummet. In bygone days, troll sweethearts would prove their love by leaping across the river, shouting out that they would love each other for the rest of their lives – which was true, as the rest of their lives lasted just as long as it took them to plunge to their deaths.

This was why in *Rubyo and Jaspilite,* the classic love story by Wollastonite Stalacspear, the final scene of the play was set at the Trollenbach Falls. To prove their love to their feuding families, the two lovers attempted to leap across the river. Rubyo slipped and fell, and Jaspilite followed her beloved to his doom. The two families came together in grief at the demise of their children, blamed each other for what had happened and continued fighting until all were dead. A typical troll story of a relationship on the rocks.

Bertram shivered. Mists of spray, rising from the invisible depths below, doused the pathway. Bertram realised that his clothes were sodden. He felt a sudden surge of elation, as if his problems were being washed away, and squared his shoulders. He wouldn't give way to despair. He wouldn't do anything as stupid as killing himself for love (and Opal probably wouldn't care a bit if he did anyway, he thought grimly). He would go back and face his problems like a troll.

But as Bertram moved away from the thunder of the falls, and retraced his steps, he heard raised voices coming from around a bend in the path. Bertram hesitated. He didn't want to meet anyone in his present mood, but there was no other way back to the city. Perhaps if he could slip by quietly, the unseen speakers would ignore him. He stepped forward cautiously – then froze as one of them came into view. Bertram recognised the bullet head and hulking form. Granite Moraine! What was *he* doing here? And who was he talking to? The other speaker remained in the shadows.

Bertram jammed his back against the cavern wall. The distant noise of the waterfall drowned out a good deal of what Granite and his unseen companion were saying, but Bertram caught a few snatches.

"Our time is coming." The voice that came out of the shadows was low rasping. Bertram was unable to tell whether it was male or female. "Our inevitable destiny is to triumph..."

"What must I do, Great Leader?" Granite was doing his best to straighten his habitual slouch into an attitude of keen anticipation. Bertram crept noiselessly forward, keeping his back pressed close to the cave wall.

"The ancient stronghold will be found," the voice continued. "Soon the great powers of our kind will arise again. You must prepare, you and your friends. The pure of heart and blood shall be rewarded. Too long, we have waited in the shadows. The doom of our enemies is at hand!"

Bertram's pulse raced and his mouth became dry. This sounded like some kind of conspiracy. Someone was going to be attacked... but who? The gobblings? The gnomes? Or was someone planning a revolution against the Trollmoot? Bertram continued to inch his silent way along the path.

Granite turned his head. A distant glow-stone made his eyes glisten and highlighted the small stream of spittle flowing from the corner of his mouth. "When's it gonna happen? When?"

"Soon." The voice became harsher. "Soon, our first blow will fall. Soon, the traitors to trollkind will be dealt with. Soon, it will be time for revenge..."

Bertram had almost stopped breathing. He still had no idea what was going on, but he had heard enough to know that if he was spotted, it would be very unhealthy for him. He edged on, past Granite, into the darkness of the tunnel. Just one more step and he would be safe! He began to move faster...

... and crashed into the muscled forms of two other trolls. Bertram ricocheted to the ground. Lying spreadeagled on the path, he looked up at the towering figures of Gabbro and Wolframite, who stared at him with unrelenting animosity.

"Granite!" bawled Gabbro. "We caught a spy!"

Within a heartbeat, the menacing form of Granite had bounded over. "Lickle Bertie. What you doin' here?" he demanded.

"I was just out for a walk," trembled Bertram.

Granite eyed him suspiciously. "What you hear?"

"Nothing, honestly. I was just walking."

Granite looked over his shoulder to the unseen companion. "What we gonna do wiv him, Great Leader?" he shouted.

For several seconds all that could be heard was the distant rumble of the mighty falls. When the command came, it was calm and measured. "There is no telling what he heard. We can take no chances. Kill him."

Bertram felt a chill in the pit of his stomach, which rippled through his body. He tried to back away, arms held out. "I didn't hear anything. Honestly, Granite. I'll just go away and forget I even saw you here."

For a moment, Granite hesitated; then his mouth set in a grim line. "You right: you ain't going to remember nothin'," he growled. "Der boss says we gotta croak you. Dere's no one to save you this time." His piggy eyes flashed maliciously and he nodded at Gabbro and Wolframite.

All three trolls closed in. Bertram tried to dodge them, to no avail. He was grabbed and scooped up off the ground. He kicked and struggled as they dragged him towards the falls, but couldn't break free from their rock-like grip. The thunder of the torrent grew. Bertram felt the scrape of the iron guard rails across his back – then there was nothing beneath him. His legs flailed as he dangled over the terrible drop.

"Please, Granite," Bertram's voice choked in desperate appeal. "You don't have to do this."

Granite's eyes flickered, but his voice was steady. "Der boss says I do."

"But I heard n
o
t
h
i
n
g
!"

Granite and his fellow thugs watched as Bertram's body disappeared into the foaming maelstrom. "He asked for it," Granite muttered.

A hooded figure stepped from the shadows. "There should have been no one here at this time. You were supposed to ensure that this place was deserted." Granite, Gabbro and Wolframite cringed. "Make sure no one else is about."

"Yes, Boss." The three trolls grovelled before the figure. Trembling, they scurried away to do its bidding.

The dark figure moved towards the edge of the falls. Two eyes gleamed out of the shadow of its hood as it gazed into the deadly abyss, but it was impossible to tell whether its expression was one of triumph – or regret.

As Bertram plummeted downwards, his only thought was, "So this is how it feels to be a lemming." But before he could start worrying about the bit where he went *splat*, his fall was interrupted by something protruding through the wall of water. He bounced upwards and an instinct for self-preservation made him reach out and grab at the rocky outcrop. His fingers tightened on it but the force of the rushing, smothering water was too great. He lost his grip and dropped down again...

...and caught at a second shelf of rock that was sticking out underneath the first. Bertram tightened his grip and held on for dear life.

Then he realised that he was no longer being drenched. He opened his eyes (which he hadn't realised were shut) and saw that the overhanging ledge above was diverting the raging water outwards. Bertram had fallen right through the torrent so that the tumbling water formed a curtain at his back and streamed down on either side. The rock to which he was clinging was comparatively dry.

"Here, watch it! You nearly had me over again!"

The unexpected voice startled Bertram so much that he nearly lost his grip. Sitting on the rocky shelf beside Bertram's right hand, with his stumpy legs dangling over the edge, was Cliff the lemming.

Bertram gaped. "I thought you were dead!"

Cliff sighed. "No such luck."

"Well, what are you doing here?"

"Preparing myself," said Cliff loftily. "Psyching myself up. Waiting for the right moment..."

"I meant what are you doing here, in this mountain, under these falls?"

The lemming glared. "Never mind that! What are *you* doing here? I mean, what a hypocrite..."

"Huh?" Bertram stared at the small, indignant creature.

"I seem to recall that you weren't in favour of throwing yourself off cliffs, landing on solid jagged rocks and going *splat* in a final sort of a way, and now look at you!" tutted Cliff. "Let me remind you, *I'm* a lemming, *you're* a troll. It's my job to throw myself off high places, not yours. And it wasn't even a good final plummet! I mean, you didn't reach the bottom! That gets you nought out of ten for style and minus several hundred for technical merit."

"But I didn't want to fall to the bottom."

Cliff eyed Bertram in astonishment. "Then what did you want to go and jump for?"

"I didn't want to! I was made to!"

"So was I, but it didn't stop you interfering."

"I'm not talking about primal urges," snapped Bertram. "I was thrown over the falls."

Cliff whistled. "You have a talent for annoying people, do you realise that?" Then a thought struck him. "Well, I suppose if you're going to leap, I could accompany you." He peered into the yawning chasm. "Mind you, it wouldn't be my personal choice, on account of the water. Still, maybe a double leap with a troll will get extra points for novelty."

"I keep telling you, I don't want to jump!"

The lemming raised an eyebrow. "Are you sure? Just let go and all your troubles will be over."

For a moment Bertram was tempted. No more worrying about where he belonged. No more feeling ashamed that he didn't fit in.

"Come on!" Cliff was becoming impatient.

"Ow!" cried Bertram. "Stop stamping on my fingers!"

"Well, get a move on. Stop hanging about!"

Bertram peered down at the raging white vortex and made his decision. "Sorry to disappoint you, but I'm not letting go."

"Oh, make your mind up!"

"Perhaps you could help me climb on to the ledge," suggested Bertram, as his hands slipped on the wet rock.

Cliff tutted. "Mr Will-He-Won't-He Troll, I'd like to point something out. I am a small creature. I probably weigh less than a medium-sized pebble. Whereas you are a hulking great thing whose weight would be closer to that of a large boulder. It won't work. You're going to have to get up here by yourself."

The lemming had a point. Calling on his troll strength, Bertram hauled himself up with agonising slowness until he lay, gasping with relief, on the rocky shelf next to Cliff. He gave a feeble grin. Cliff smiled uncertainly in return.

Then Bertram remembered where they were. "How did you get here anyway?" he asked.

Cliff shrugged. "It's all your fault. You completely put me

off the whole leaping-off-a-mountain thing. So I followed you inside it instead. Thought I might find a nice pothole or shaft to throw myself down. You know, for a change."

"And you didn't find one?"

Cliff shuffled his feet evasively. "Well – not a *suitable* one. Not one that *felt* right."

Bertram nodded. "I see."

"But I found a secret passage that led to a hidden cave that led to this ledge."

"What hidden cave?"

"That one." The lemming pointed at an opening in the rocky wall behind them.

Bertram stared in disbelief. "I didn't know there was a hidden cave that led here."

"Maybe because it's hidden," replied Cliff, with more than a hint of sarcasm. "Anyway, you still haven't told me what *you're* doing here."

"I told you. I was thrown over the falls."

Cliff sighed. "Aren't you the lucky one. I wish I could get someone to do that for me. It'd take out the decision-making process."

Bertram walked unsteadily across the ledge and peered into the hidden cave. Just inside, a passage opened out to the right, leading downwards. Bertram sniffed. The air from this passage smelt fresh and clean. "Where does this lead to?"

"To the outside world," said Cliff promptly. "But there's another..."

"The outside world!" Bertram tried to marshal his

confused, sluggish thoughts into some sort of order. He was sure of only one thing: if he stepped into this tunnel, there would be no going back.

What would his mother think about his disappearance? Should he try to let her know that he was all right, or was it best he simply vanish? That way he wouldn't bring any more misery on her. Nobody else would care. Bertram was sure Opal and her uncle wouldn't miss him. Opal thought he was a wash-out – and Councillor Shale knew that Bertram wasn't really a proper troll.

"I'm not going back," he said aloud.

"Oh," said Cliff. "Right. You want me to show you the way out?" Bertram nodded decisively. "This way," the lemming said jauntily, setting off down the passage at a steady trot. "Please proceed in an orderly fashion, no running, bumping or barging..."

Bertram followed his small guide into the darkness.

As they scrambled through the deep, cold, dripping caverns with Cliff, Bertram told the lemming his sorry story.

"I can't believe those trolls tried to kill you!" Cliff exclaimed indignantly. "Why don't you go back to Caer Borundum and give 'em what for? That Councillor Wossisface'd soon sort them out."

Bertram shook his head. "But then my secret would come out..."

The lemming's ears pricked up. "What secret?"

Bertram looked away from Cliff. "I'm not really a troll."

Cliff eyed his companion suspiciously. "Go on! You look like a troll to me!"

"I'm half-human. If the other trolls found out, they'd start treating my mother the way they've always treated me. No. It's better if they think I'm dead. I'll just have to go and live somewhere else."

Cliff nodded. "I know what you mean. The other lemmings are starting to give me funny looks. I don't see what business it is of theirs if I decide to take my time about going *splat*. Still, it's not very nice."

At long last, the companions emerged from a cleft in the rocks on to the windswept mountainside. Above them the moon and stars shimmered in the grey-blue sky. Bertram breathed in the crisp night air. Below them moors and meadows stretched to a distant line of dark green. A wild bird called *kwok-kok-kok*, but to Bertram the call now sounded like *go back – back – back*! He paused, irresolute.

Cliff cleared his throat. "You know, we're migratory, us lemmings. We get about a bit. That green line beyond the moors, that's the Forest – The Dark Forest. It goes on and on to the end of the world. And somewhere in it, far to the south, there's a human city. It's called Dun Indewood."

Bertram shrugged. "So what?"

"You're half-troll, half-human," Cliff pointed out with a meaningful look. "The trolls think you're dead. Why not try your luck with the humans?"

Bertram thought about this. Since Granite had thrown

him over the falls, trying his luck with humans didn't sound such a crazy idea after all.

"Of course," said Cliff hastily, "I might not be able to come with you the whole way, on account of I'm planning to throw myself off something very tall, very soon..."

Bertram gave Cliff the ghost of a smile. "But until then, you're saying we could stick together?"

The lemming nodded and returned Bertram's hesitant grin. "If you like."

So placing Cliff on one broad shoulder, Bertram set off down the mountain, heading towards a new life and a destiny that he could never have imagined.

Book The Second

The Book of The Wanderer

(The Two Powers)

Chapter One

How Bertram Dealt with a Thorny Problem and Coped with a Challenging Situation.

Bertram and Cliff tramped over the lonely moors at the foot of Mount Ynside. The mountain diminished behind them and the line of trees that marked the start of the Dark Forest grew ever closer.

Few creatures lived on the moors. They saw hares and the occasional deer, and from time to time the sound of their approach sent fat birds rocketing skywards with whirring wings and hysterical cries. At night, Bertram curled up on the springy moss or made himself a bed in the heather, with Cliff sleeping in the crook of his arm. Bertram had started with a vague notion that he ought to do the troll-like thing and travel by night, but after he and Cliff had been misled by Will o' the Wisps, and fallen into bogs a few times, they decided that daytime travel was more practical.

Before long they left the moors behind, crossed the meadows where wild goats grazed on the tussocky grasses, and found themselves in the Dark Forest.

Bertram was surprised to find that the Forest was, in some ways, similar to the world of the trolls. Vines hung from branches like stalactites, anthills mushroomed from the Forest floor like stalagmites. Streams rushed gurgling through the Forest, just as they did in the mountain. In many places the ancient trees, choked with ivy and dripping with moss, blotted out the sun almost as effectively as the rock of Mount Ynside. Elsewhere they spread out to reveal clearings, just as the tunnels of Bertram's former home opened out into caverns.

From time to time, the briars, bushes and brambles of the Forest floor blocked the travellers' path as completely as any rockfall, and Cliff and Bertram were forced to use assorted trackways that rambled between the denser thickets. Presumably these had been made by animals – bears, perhaps, or wild boar; or maybe the mysterious hunters that stalked the travellers, their unseen bodies rustling bushes by day and their glowing eyes peering disturbingly from the undergrowth by night.

Cliff was turning out to be a difficult travelling companion. He kept finding improbable ways to try and obey his lemming instincts. These were always completely unsuccessful, but they often caused trouble and delay.

When he wasn't finding novel methods to end it all, the lemming kept up a constant stream of chatter that tried Bertram's patience sorely.

The Dark Forest made Bertram uneasy. However close the trees pressed, they weren't quite like the comfortingly solid caves of home. The leaf mould of the Forest floor felt nauseatingly soft and yielding compared to the rocky floors of Caer Borundum. The sound of the wind in the trees and the cries of creatures and birds were nothing like the gentle murmur of the air currents in the tunnels, the soft grunting of draught-moles and the shrill chittering of bats. But to Bertram's relief, the unseen denizens of the Dark Forest seemed to be wary of creatures as large as trolls and for the most part prudently stayed out of the way.

Days passed into weeks, weeks into months, and the companions journeyed on. They kept the sunrise on their left and the sunset on their right, travelling ever south through the Dark Forest.

Many tales are told of Bertram's epic journey with Cliff the lemming from Caer Borundum to the City of Dun Indewood. Some of them are even true.

The Tale of Bertram and the Sleeping Castle

After countless weeks of travel, Bertram and Cliff found their path blocked by a huge wall of thorns. The briars stretched as far as the eye could see.

"Interesting," said Bertram, stepping forward and pulling

at one of the thick, green branches. "Ow! These thorns are sharp!" He sucked his thumb.

Cliff snorted. "Well, leave them alone then! If you go picking at sharp objects, what do you expect?"

"I'm trying to find us a way through," replied Bertram.

"We don't *have* to find a way through," Cliff pointed out. "We could just walk round. Admittedly, it could be a bit of a detour, but what's a few extra miles on top of the hundreds we've already covered?"

Ignoring the lemming, Bertram pulled at another tangle of tough, unyielding briars. "I think there's a castle behind all this stuff."

"What's a castle? And how do you know it is one?"

"They're stone things humans build to live in when they can't find a cave," replied Bertram. "When I was young, my mother used to read old fairy-slates to me. There were always pictures of castles and knights and witches."

"Well, how do you know there's one in here?" demanded Cliff.

Bertram wriggled through the gap he had made. "You can see the turrets sticking out."

"All right, granted there's a castle, does that mean we have to tear the skin off our paws trying to get in? What do you expect to find in there anyway? Like you said, it probably belongs to a witch." Cliff warmed to his theme. "Yes, that's it, a witch who doesn't want to be disturbed, so she puts an enchantment on the castle to make briars and brambles and thorn trees grow up all around it so nobody can get in and disturb her. Except for a certain pigheaded troll who hasn't got the sense to leave well alone, and who is probably very shortly going to be turned into a newt..." Cliff paused as a thought struck him. "What are turrets?"

"Sort of towers, sticking out of the highest part of the castle."

"So they're high turrets?" said Cliff in a casual voice. "The sort that, if one was so minded, one could jump off with a reasonable expectation of going *splat*?"

Bertram moaned. "Here we go again."

Cliff glared. "What do you expect? You know I'm going to end it all..."

"No, you're not!" said Bertram heatedly. "You're not because we've been walking through this Forest for ages now and you haven't done it yet, so you're not going to do it. You don't really want to. It's just attention-seeking, that's all."

Cliff almost gobbled with rage. "I like that! I keep trying to end my miserable existence and what happens? An interfering troll keeps rescuing me. Remember when I threw myself into that volcano...?"

"It was extinct."

"Well, I didn't know that! What about when I tried to drown myself?"

"In a puddle."

"It was a pond! A very *big* pond! And then those sharks came..."

"They were sticklebacks."

"Size is relative, Mister Big Troll. When you're my size, a stickleback is a..."

"...small fish whose diet does not include lemmings."

"All right!" Cliff stood with his paws on his hips, looking daggers at Bertram. "What about when I threw myself out of that tree...?"

"Bush." Bertram renewed his attack on the thorns.

"...and then I picked a fight with that weasel..."

"Vole. You were twice his weight."

"Do you remember when we met that ghoul? I practically begged him to eat me!"

"Knowing perfectly well," said Bertram wearily, "that ghouls only eat dead things. It's pathetic. Especially when you try to get me to help you. Like when we built that campfire. You only had to light it while I went to get water. When I got back I found you'd made a spit and tied yourself to it, and you were hanging over the wood shouting, 'Go on, baste me, you know you want to! Come on, Bertie, light my pyre!'"

"My point exactly!" cried Cliff triumphantly. "A clear demonstration of my authentic, lemming-like determination to do myself in! You were impressed! Admit it!"

"I might have been, if you'd lit the fire first."

"You could have lit it, instead of untying me," said Cliff accusingly. "You just don't want to help."

"No, I don't." Bertram hauled a thorn bush out of the ground, roots and all. "Aha!" He dragged aside a final tangle of branches to reveal the rough stones of a castle wall.

"Well done!" sneered Cliff. "Of course, from the point of view of getting into the castle, a door would be about a hundred times more useful. Just how do you think you're going to get through that wall?"

Bertram clenched his fists and swung. When masonry had stopped falling, Cliff commented, "Ah. The troll approach to problem-solving. Let's hope the owners aren't too house-proud."

Bertram gave the lemming a withering glance and stepped through the gap he had smashed. Muttering, Cliff followed. Together, they walked through a courtyard and into the castle.

Cliff whistled. "This place is way overdue for spring-cleaning."

The whole castle lay still and silent. Everything was covered with a thick layer of dust, including the people. There were bodies all over the place, their chests rising and falling in a steady rhythm and their eyes closed. Guards drooped over their spears. A baker lay with his head pillowed on a tray of bread. A cook and a butler sat back-to-back, supporting each other and snoring loudly.

Bertram gazed curiously about. "Are these *people*?"

Cliff kicked the guard. "What else would they be?"

"I mean, are they human? I've never seen a human in real life, only in pictures."

Cliff gave a derisive snort and said, "Of course they are."

Bertram shook his head in wonderment. "They don't look evil."

"Who said they were?"

"Well, Councillor Shale said humans put the Man-curse on us trolls, so I assumed they must be." Shaking his head, Bertram marched towards the door leading into the great hall. Cliff watched him go. Then he turned and cast a speculative eye at a spiral staircase which led temptingly upwards...

The great hall was littered with men, women and children, all dressed in fine clothes, all asleep. At the far end, a man and a woman, each wearing a heavy-looking gold crown, sprawled across beautifully crafted thrones thick with spiders' webs. On a table before them lay a crystal casket. And in the casket...

Bertram caught his breath. In the casket lay a girl. Even to a troll who had never seen a human, she was obviously a girl. A beautiful human girl.

He recalled one of the fairy-slates his mother had read to him. "This girl is a princess," he said softly to himself, "and she's been put under a spell by a wicked witch..." Bertram felt himself go hot and cold all over. "And she will remain in her enchanted sleep until she is awoken... by... a kiss..."

Slowly, hesitantly, Bertram bent over the casket.

"Hey, Mister Unhelpful Troll! Up here!"

Distracted, Bertram glanced up to find the source of the tiny, distant voice. Cliff was perched on a ledge high above the great hall. The lemming waved. His voice floated down to Bertram. "Look – I've found the perfect spot to cast myself to my doom! And you can watch!"

Bertram raised his arms in protest. "Nooooooo!"

The lemming jumped.

Bertram strode through the Dark Forest, moodily kicking small trees out of the way. Cliff had to run to keep up. "My fault?" he panted. "My fault? How is what happened my fault?"

The troll strode on. "Shut up."

"I mean, imagine you're a princess – gentle upbringing, sheltered life, occasional bit of spinning – and you're put into an enchanted sleep for a hundred years, and when you wake up, you're expecting Prince Charming. And what do you see instead? An ugly great troll bending over you making kissy-faces! Naturally, you're going to scream the place down."

"Shut up."

"And then, just as naturally, the king and queen and all the courtiers are going to wake up and find a troll making goo-goo eyes at their precious daughter and call for the guards!"

Bertram stopped and swung round on the lemming. "Excuse me! Just who woke the princess up? Did I wake her with a kiss? I don't think so. Did a lemming with an underdeveloped death wish hurl himself from a high balcony and land on her stomach? Why, I believe it did!" He turned and stomped off again.

"I was aiming for the edge of the table," protested Cliff.

"Of course you were."

"I just forgot about allowing for wind speed."

"There was no wind – we were inside a castle!"

"I know. That's why I shouldn't have allowed for it."

"Shut up!"

"How do we get across?" said Cliff, staring at the river before them. "Maybe you can swim over and I'll perch on your back, giving you encouragement."

"And you won't accidentally-on-purpose slip off and try to drown yourself?"

"I might," conceded Cliff.

"Anyway, I don't do swimming. You know that." Bertram thought for a moment. "We'll walk downriver. There may be a bridge or a crossing point somewhere." He set off along the riverbank.

Sure enough, a few miles downstream Bertram found what he was looking for: a ford. "We can cross here. It looks safe enough."

"Spoilsport." Cliff stared at a small clearing beside the ford. "What's that tent thing doing there? With the horse outside? And why's that shield hanging in that tree?"

"I don't know," said Bertram thoughtfully. "Perhaps I'm supposed to bang on it. You know? To let somebody know we're here?"

"Who?"

"Well, we won't know until I bang on it, will we?"

Bertram banged on the shield and dented it. It fell out of the tree.

"Righto – hang on! Don't go away! With you in a minute!" A muffled voice sounded from inside the tent. There was a lot of clattering and the voice muttered to itself, "Now where did I put those pauldrons? And my gorget? Oh, this place is a pigsty..."

After some minutes, a man staggered out of the tent. He was wearing black armour. As he pulled on a gauntlet, he tripped over a tree root and the visor on his helmet shut with a snap.

"Blast!" he said. "Now then, how does it go? Got it... got it..." He raised his voice and cried, "Stand, vile recreant, and seek not to pass this way or thou must adventure arms against the Black Knyght."

Bertram stared at the Black Knyght. "I beg your pardon?"

The Black Knyght had reached his horse and managed to get one foot in the stirrup. He was now hopping frantically on the other foot as the horse walked sedately round in a circle. "I have sworn – *keep still, you stupid animal* – to defend this passage of the river against all who journey this way. So defend thyself, Sir Knyght... Aha!" With a grunt of triumph, the Black Knyght succeeded in getting astride his horse. "Now, Sir Knyght," he cried, "keep thee well, thou wert best, for I will slay thee, maugre thy head." He managed to get his visor open. "Stone the crows!"

Bertram regarded him with interest. "*What* my head?"

The Black Knyght realised for the first time that he was not talking to a normal human. Although he was on horseback, his eyes were level with Bertram's. "Here, what are you standing on?"

Bertram looked down at his feet, puzzled. "Nothing."

"Oh, gra'mercy." The Black Knyght began to tremble so hard his armour rattled. A rivet popped out.

"You said you were going to slay me, *something* my head. What did you mean?"

The Black Knyght's voice shook. "*M-maugre* thy head. It's a... sort of... threat. It means, 'and you can't stop me, so there'. More or less."

"Oh," said Bertram. "Why do you want to slay me?"

"Well, I took an oath, you see, to hold the ford against all comers – so every time a Knyght comes along to cross the ford, I fight him and take his armour and throw him in prison, you see..."

Bertram considered this curious custom. "And how many Knyghts have you fought so far?" he asked.

The Black Knyght looked sheepish. "Well, so far – none. It's a very quiet ford."

Bertram shrugged. "All right then." He began to roll up his sleeves.

The Black Knyght shot him a look of pure terror. "W-what are you doing?"

"You said you wanted to fight me. I thought we'd better get on with it."

The Black Knyght's teeth started chattering. "Well, I didn't mean I want to fight *you*, obviously."

"But I want to cross the ford," Bertram pointed out mildly. "That's the way to Dun Indewood, isn't it?"

"Ah, yes, but you see..." The Black Knyght seemed at a loss. Then he clicked his armoured fingers and said hurriedly, "But my oath was only to fight Knyghts, and you're not a Knyght." He folded his arms triumphantly.

"Oh," said Bertram. "Aren't I? How do you know?"

The Black Knyght gave a nervous chuckle. "Well, because you haven't got any armour... or a sword, or a lance, or a charger... and in any case, Knyghts aren't usually ten feet tall and built like a brick privy, and they're not usually..." The Black Knyght realised that Bertram was watching him with a certain quiet intensity. "Grey..." he heard himself saying.

Bertram was feeling tired and irritable. He had walked a long way. His feet hurt. "Grey?" he said softly. "You don't like grey?"

"I love grey!" The Black Knyght's voice became a panic-stricken squeak. "Grey is terrific! It works with everything! Some of my best friends are grey. Cross the ford! Go ahead! Be my guest! Bring a friend!"

"Have at thee, Sir Knyght!"

The Black Knyght jumped, and looked around in bafflement at the sound of this new voice.

"Down here, you fool!"

The Black Knyght stared down. There, between the giant, grey monster and his horse, was a small, furry creature. It was windmilling clenched paws in front of its tiny face and dancing backwards and forwards, making strange, sniffing noises.

"Come on then, put 'em up!" Cliff did a sideways shuffle. "Pick on someone your own size. I'll tear you limb from limb with my bare paws. Come on, what are you afraid of? You've got a horse and armour and a sword and everything. You want a piece of me? Bring it on!"

Bertram stared down at Cliff with pained disapproval. "You're making yourself look ridiculous."

"Stay out of this, big fella. This is between me and Mister Rusty here."

"You're just trying to get yourself killed again. It's pathetic and childish. I've told you before, it's just a cry for help..."

"If that walking tin-can gets off his horse, we'll see who cries for help!"

Bertram gave the Black Knyght an apologetic look. "I'm sorry about this. Will you please tell him you don't want to fight him?"

The Black Knyght's self-control snapped. "Fight him? Of course I don't want to fight him! I took an oath to fight Knyghts in honourable single combat. Nobody said anything about fighting stupid guinea pigs and ugly, grey trolls..." The Black Knyght's voice faltered and died away.

Cliff narrowed his eyes. "*Guinea pig?*"

So did Bertram. "*Ugly?*"

Sometime later, Bertram and Cliff were walking through the Dark Forest.

"You might have carried me over that stream," the lemming complained.

"Shut up."

"My fur is *sopping*."

"Shut up."

"And as for what you did to that poor Knyght. He was only doing his job. Probably quite a nice chap when you got to know him," said Cliff.

"Oh, really?" replied Bertram. "Was that why you went up the leg of his armour? On the inside? Just before he turned purple and started screaming?"

"Well, at least I didn't squeeze him so hard that he shot out of the top of his armour and ended up in the ford," Cliff retorted.

"I was just trying to get *you* out."

There was a long silence.

Bertram glanced down at Cliff. The lemming was striding along in a determined fashion with his cheeks puffed out and his eyes popping. "What are you doing now?"

"I'm holding my breath. Well, I was. Up until then, because I had to take a breath to say that. But when I've finished saying this, I shall do it again. If I do it for long enough, I'll be a gonner and you can't stop me. What do you think of *that*, Mister Clever Troll?"

"Shut up."

Chapter Two

How Bertram's Playmate Went Up in the World and Cliff narrowly avoided Becoming a Picnic.

There were now more signs of human habitation in the Dark Forest. Bertram and Cliff had been skirting around isolated homesteads and scattered hamlets for several days.

"We must be getting near the City of Dun Indewood. Why don't you have another go at meeting some humans? You've got to try sometime if you're ever going to be friends with them," Cliff pointed out crossly as he clambered through a dense thicket in order to avoid a forester's cottage.

Bertram shrugged unhappily. "I suppose so – but my meetings with humans haven't been very successful so far..."

He was interrupted by the sound of singing, drifting through the trees.

"See-saw
Margewy Daw
Johnny will have a new ma-sta..."

"That's it!" Cliff danced a little jig. "That's never an adult human voice. It must be a child. I bet children won't be as scared of you as grown-ups. If you make friends, she can tell the grown-ups about you and sort of get them used to the idea."

"Do you think that will work?" asked Bertram anxiously.

"Bound to," said Cliff, crossing his claws for luck.

The companions moved cautiously towards the source of the singing. Tiptoeing their way through the trees, they arrived at a small clearing.

Before them, in the middle of the grassy glade, was the forester's tumbledown cottage. Smoke spiralled skywards from the chimney poking out of its thatched roof. Smells of cooking wafted on the lazy afternoon air.

In front of the cottage was a small barrel lying on its side. Balanced over it was a long wooden plank and sitting astride one end of the makeshift seesaw was a small child. She wore a blue petticoat and a linen jacket. Her freckled face peered out from a mass of strawberry-blonde hair.

"See-saw
Margewy Daw

Johnny will have a new ma-sta.
He can earn but a penny a day
Because he can't work any fa-sta!"

Bertram sniffed at the air. "It seems like for ever since I had a cooked meal."

Cliff's demeanour brightened. "Maybe they could cook me! Roast lemming, served with a few vegetables and a dash of gravy. Or as a dessert. I'd make a wonderful lemming meringue pie!"

Bertram gave Cliff his best stony glare before stepping out into the glade.

"See-saw,
Margewy..."

The child stopped mid-song and stared wide-eyed at Bertram. He gave a toothy grin and waved. Cliff followed Bertram's friendly example. The girl's face dissolved into a dimpled smile and she chuckled.

Bertram returned the laugh and gave Cliff a "I-think-it's-going-to-be-all-right" nod of the head.

"Hello, monsta."

Bertram held out his hands and stepped forward. "I'm not a monster," he said, "I'm Bertram."

"Hello, Bertwam the monsta."

A female voice called out from inside the cottage. "Who are you talking to, Sophia?"

"A monsta," replied the small girl. "He's called Bertwam."

"That's nice, dear."

Sophia smiled at Bertram. "That's my mummy. She's cooking gingerbwead."

"Yum, yum," replied Bertram wondering what gingerbwead was. He gestured towards Cliff. "This is my friend."

The little girl made a face. "Yeurk! It's a wat!"

"A wat?" puzzled Bertram. "What's a wat?"

"That's a wat." Sophia pointed at Cliff. "Your fwend's a wat."

Cliff shook a bristling paw. "I'm not a wat... I mean, rat. I'm a lemming."

"A lemming?" Sophia shook her head. "Lemmings aren't fuwwy. Lemmings are yellow and taste howwible and they don't talk. You're a wat and that's that!"

Bertram stifled a giggle. "His name is Cliff."

"Hello, Cliff the wat. I'm Sophia. You can be my fwend too."

Friends! Bertram grinned down at Cliff. "We've made friends with a human!"

"A rat," muttered Cliff. "I ask you, a rat!"

"Monsta, will you play see-saw wiv me? It's no fun playing on my own, because there's no one to saw when I see, or see when I saw, see?"

Bertram stared at the wooden contraption before him. "What do I do?" he asked.

Sophia giggled. "Silly monsta, not knowing how to see-saw! You sit on the other end of the plank and we take it in turns to bounce up and down and we sing *See-saw Margewy Daw.*"

"That sounds fun!" Bertram moved to the raised end of the plank.

Realisation suddenly hit Cliff. "I don't think that's a good idea."

"Oh, come on. 'Make friends with humans', you said."

"Yes, but..."

Without further delay, Bertram vaulted enthusiastically on to the end of the plank. Sophia shot skywards with a scream.

Her mother's voice wafted from the cottage. "Play quietly with the monster, dear."

Cliff followed the little girl's looping flight with interest. "I didn't realise humans could fly," he said. "Birds do it better. Humans do too much wailing and not enough flapping of the arms."

Bertram stared at the still ascending figure in horrified disbelief.

"Look, she's going right over those unbelievably tall trees," added Cliff. "Very impressive!"

"I didn't mean that to happen," protested Bertram, as the distant figure disappeared from sight.

"Well, don't worry," soothed the lemming. "I'm sure her parents will find her... eventually."

There was a loud splash followed by the sound of shrieking.

"Sounds like she's found a soft landing," mused Cliff. "I hope she can swim."

Bertram gave Cliff an apprehensive look as the child's wails split the forest air. "Do you think we should go and explain what happened?"

"No," replied Cliff thoughtfully. "I think we should run away."

"I think you're right."

"Everything is going wrong!" moaned Bertram sometime later as he and Cliff stopped to catch their breath. "Maybe it was a mistake to come looking for humans."

"Well, it hasn't gone well so far," agreed Cliff.

Bertram plodded on disconsolately, grumbling. "I don't belong in the troll world; I don't belong in the human world. I'm half and half and it just adds up to nothing."

"You're wrong on the arithmetic front," interjected Cliff. "I think you'll find that two halves add up to one."

"Life," sighed Bertram despondently. "What a game!"

Cliff nodded wisely. "Yep. In your case, it's a game of two halves."

Bertram flopped on to the Forest floor and leant against a tree (which creaked alarmingly), the picture of misery.

Cliff sprang on to a fallen tree trunk and looked Bertram in the eye. "The problem with you is that you think about yourself too much!" he exclaimed. "Me, me, me! Hah! You think you've got problems. What about thinking about others for a change?"

"Like who?"

"Like me! Here am I, trying to do what all good lemmings should, and you keep stopping me from fulfilling my destiny.

You won't set fire to me or throw me off a tower or launch me into space. Oh, no, you'll do it to others, but not me. I help to save your life and you repay it by trying to save mine. No wonder you can't get on with anyone. You're just selfish."

Bertram was stung by Cliff's attack. "Selfish? I spend all my time watching out for you! Perhaps if I wasn't lumbered with a death-wish rodent, I might be able to get on in the human world just a little better!"

"Oh!" cried Cliff, "Oh! It's all my fault, is it?"

"Yes!" roared Bertram, jumping to his feet. "I'd be a lot better off without you."

Cliff bristled. "Right, Mr Me-me-me Troll, if that's what you want, you've got it! I'm off!" The lemming began to stamp off down the track. "I don't need you to hold my paw for me. I can manage well enough on my own."

"Good!" Bertram stormed off in the opposite direction.

"I'll show him," muttered the lemming. "I don't need him to help me fulfil my destiny." He kicked savagely at a fallen fir cone. "Not that he would anyway. He could have just accidentally-on-purpose not looked behind him and sat on me and squashed me flat any time he wanted, but did he? Oh, no."

Cliff continued down the path muttering and grumbling while the shadows of the trees lengthened and the air began to turn chill. At length, he stopped and looked upwards.

"Trees all around me," he moaned. "*Tall* trees. Tall, *unclimbable* trees. What a waste! It's enough to make a lemming weep." Still looking up, Cliff took a step back – and bumped into something. Turning round, he discovered it was a very dirty, hairy leg.

"Well, hellooo there!"

The creature looming over the lemming was wearing the remnants of a frock coat and a linen shirt. Tufts of grey fur poked out through numerous holes. It held a battered three-cornered hat in its left paw and its right eye twitched.

Cliff had never encountered such a creature before. "What are you?" he asked in an interested sort of way.

"I am a highwaywolf," replied the creature, bowing low. "I am a rogue of the open road – a dark, dashing, romantic vagabond, lauded by poets and acclaimed by minstrels."

Cliff eyed the wolf's attire. "You don't look very dashing."

The wolf's eye twitched again. "Things haven't been going too well recently. However..." The beast licked its lips. "...it seems that the situation is looking up. You would make a nice little appetiser before I get on to, hmmm... meatier victims."

Cliff's face brightened. "Oh, you're going to *eat* me!"

The wolf nodded. "That is the general idea."

"Great! I knew I didn't need that lumbering troll."

The wolf looked puzzled.

"Well, let's get on with it." Cliff lay on the ground with his paws across his chest. "Got any seasoning with you? Salt? Pepper? Garlic? I'd go really nicely with a clove of garlic – maybe a sprig of parsley for decoration..."

"No, it isn't really necessary. *Au naturel* will be fine."

"Ah, well, I daresay you're the expert."

The wolf picked up Cliff and ogled him.

Cliff gulped. "What big eyes you've got."

"All the better to see small things like you," replied the wolf. "And don't tell me I've got big ears as well." It shuddered. "I've heard it all before."

"Well, you *have* got big ears," said Cliff defiantly.

"Oh, well, if you insist. All the better to hear your agonised squeals." The wolf took a deep, satisfied breath and opened its slavering mouth. "Now, were you going to say something about my teeth?"

"Yes – well, they're pretty big as well." Cliff's voice wavered.

"All the better to eat you with!" The wolf licked its chops expectantly. "Now that we've got the formalities over with... yum-yum." Its terrible jaws gaped wide.

Cliff closed his eyes and trembled. "*Bon appétit,*" he said faintly.

"I wouldn't do that if I were you."

The wolf's paw was suddenly caught in an iron grip. The shocked creature paused mid-drool and stared at the grey hand that held him. Then its gaze wandered up a heavily muscled arm and settled on a huge, disapproving face.

"Oh, not again!" complained Cliff, trying very hard to keep the relief out of his voice.

"Do you know this... thing?" the wolf asked Cliff, as Bertram prised the lemming from his grasp.

Bertram placed Cliff on a high branch; then he thought better of this and removed him to a lower one. Seeing the troll preoccupied, the wolf took his chance and pounced.

"Look out!" warned Cliff.

Bertram spun round. The wolf's teeth closed on his arm.

There was a crunching sound followed by a short silence. A look of pained astonishment spread over the wolf's face. It loosened its grip on Bertram's arm and its teeth loosened themselves from its gums. They dropped to the ground with sad little plinking sounds.

"Oh gy teef," moaned the wolf. "Look what you've gun to gy teef!" It scrabbled on the ground, frantically collecting its broken fangs.

Cliff scowled at Bertram. "That's the second time I've saved your life! If I hadn't shouted out that warning, it would have eaten you."

"Well, it might have gummed me to death," conceded Bertram.

"So why did you come back?" demanded the lemming.

Bertram gave a cough. "I thought you might be in danger."

"Chance would be a fine thing. So you come running back, ruining things again, saving me without a by-your-leave..." Cliff folded his paws across his chest and sulked.

The wolf held his displaced teeth in cupped paws and raised an agonised face to Bertram. "Fang you very much!" it wailed. "Whak gig you go an' goo gat for?" It nodded towards Cliff. "How am I schupposhed to eak him now?"

Bertram wagged a finger under the wolf's nose. "This lemming is my friend. You're not to eat the lemming."

"Eak him?" The wolf gave a despairing moan. "I coulgn't eak him now unlesh he wash lemming shquash. Or shoup—"

A hoarse voice interrupted from the side of the path: "Tough luck, wolfie."

The wolf's right eye resumed its twitching. "Oh, no. Gak's all I neeg!"

A group of tough-looking men armed with bows and swords stepped out of the bushes. They were wearing green tunics and cloaks pinned with shiny copper badges.

"'Ullo, chummy." The oldest and most villainous-looking member of the group shook his head sorrowfully. "Dear oh dear. Up to your old tricks again?"

The wolf gave the speaker a disgusted stare. "I liked you bekker when you were the King of Thieves."

"Ah, but I ain't a thief no more." The man grinned at the wolf and nodded towards his men. "None of us is. We're Forest Rangers in the service of the High Lord of Dun Indewood – popularly known as Badgers." The man patted his badge and gave the wolf an outrageous wink. "So make yourself scarce before I arrest you for attempted picnicking out of season and conspiring to eat Forest creatures without due care and attention."

With a howl of despair, the wolf plunged into the dense undergrowth and vanished from sight. A couple of the Badgers playfully loosed their arrows after it to speed it on its way.

Bertram bowed politely to the leader of the Badgers. "Thank you – but we weren't in any danger."

"Maybe you was and maybe you wasn't." The ex-King of Thieves leered at Bertram and Cliff. "But you are now. We've been followin' you ever since you came close to Dun Indewood."

"Dun Indewood!" exclaimed Bertram. "We've arrived!"

The ex-King of Thieves raised an eyebrow. "So you *are*

heading for the City. Well, High Lord Robat don't like strangers snoopin' round wivout 'is permission. We ain't rescuin' you. We're arrestin' you."

Bertram weighed up his opponents. "What if I don't want to be arrested?" he asked, flexing his muscles in a pointed manner.

Suddenly, a dozen arrow points were trained on Cliff.

"Then," the ex-King of Thieves said, "the little furry fing gets it."

Cliff beamed.

Bertram sighed. "Lead on."

Chapter Three

Of Inquestigators, Pastafarians and Rock Cakes.

The moment he entered Dun Indewood, Bertram's senses were overpowered by an explosion of sounds, sights and smells.

The City Square just inside the North Gate was choked with a hurly-burly of humans wearing such brightly coloured clothes that Bertram (who was used to dark troll-garments) felt his eyes start to ache. Cattle in their pens, chickens and ducks in wicker baskets, geese and sheep in flocks, and pigs snuffling in the gutters added their calls to the street vendors' cries to produce a great cacophony.

Prompted by the Badgers, Bertram, with Cliff on his

shoulder, stepped out of the shadow of the gatehouse. The noise stopped instantly as every eye was turned on them. Bertram gave a sheepish grin and waved nervously. Cliff glared at the silent crowds. "What's the matter? You never seen a lemming before?"

Then the pointing and muttering began.

"It's a giant!"

"No, it's an ogre."

"Ogres are green. That's a troll."

"A troll! We'll be murdered in our beds!"

"What's a lemming?"

The same scenario was enacted over and over again as Bertram and his escort passed through the crowded streets of Dun Indewood, pursued by fearful looks and dark mutterings. Bertram was quite relieved when they reached the Castle of Dun Indewood, away from the staring eyes and the mutterings of the citizens, and were shepherded into the Armoury. Here swords, lances, pikes, daggers, longbows and arrows, crossbows and quarrels, clung to the wall in neat circles, pointing inwards. At the centre of each circle hung crossed axes, maces and morningstars. The effect was cheerfully barbaric.

The Badgers took up station around the walls of the room, lolling about in attitudes of unconvincing nonchalance. Their swords were sheathed, but loosely, and those holding crossbows were swinging them carelessly, but the safety catches were off. Bertram and Cliff were motioned to sit on a bench facing a small gnome-like creature who was sitting the wrong way round on a chair with his arms folded across its back. Behind him, an old man sat at a table. He was looking, not at the newcomers, but at a number of carved stone counters. From time to time he would throw these across the table top and study them closely before gathering them up and repeating the process.

The smaller figure gave Bertram and Cliff a ferocious grin. "Humfrey the Boggart, Chief Inqueshtigator of the City of Dun Indewood. Shupposhe you guysh tell me what you're doin' here?"

There followed a string of questions: Who were they? Where had they come from? Where were they going? Where had they been on the night of the fourteenth? Bertram answered these questions as honestly as he could. Eventually, Humfrey seemed to run out of things to ask and sat staring up at Bertram, clearly at a loss.

"We don't get many trollsh in Dun Indewood," he said. "Ash a matter of fact, we've never had *any* trollsh here for yearsh."

Bertram gave Humfrey an offended look. "I'm not surprised, if you set your guards on them the minute they stick their noses out of the Forest."

Humfrey scratched his head. "That ishn't exactly what I meant..." He looked towards his companion, but the old man was still poring intently over his stone counters. "I mean," the boggart continued, "we get all shortsh here – humansh, gnomesh, elvesh, even bansheesh..."

Bertram's head spun as he tried to get his ears around Humfrey's bizarre pronunciation. "Bansheesh?"

"I think he means banshees," said Cliff helpfully. "They

look like old women with long hair. They wear grey cloaks and green dresses, and their eyes are red with weeping, and when someone's going to die they go *Aaaiiiieeeeeeeeee!*" The lemming let out a blood-curdling wail. Humfrey turned pale and nearly fell off his chair.

Bertram stared at Cliff. "You're very well-informed about banshees."

Cliff gave a superior sniff. "Lemmings know a lot about death-spirits. Why should that be a surprise?" The small creature gazed admiringly at the weapons on display. "Wow! Some of those knives look really sharp..."

"Stop it." Bertram poked a gigantic finger in the lemming's furry belly.

"Killjoy."

Humfrey rubbed at the corners of his mouth. "There'sh a couple of thingsh worrying me. Firshtly, trollsh and humansh are deadly enemiesh – sho what'sh a troll doing wanting to live among humansh?" The boggart shook his head. "And shecondly, ash far ash I know, any troll that'sh caught above ground in daylight getsh turned to shtone. Sho how come we ain't calling you Rocky?"

Bertram shrugged. "I suppose it's because I'm only half a troll. My father was human."

There was a clatter from the table behind Humfrey. The old man sitting there had leapt to his feet. This sudden move had sent the carved stone counters skittering across the table top. Bertram eyed them with interest.

Humfrey tutted. "Hey, Runie. You wanna be careful with thoshe thingsh! How are you gonna prophecy the future if half your runeshtonesh end up in the log bashket or down the back of the shofa?"

The Runemaster, Chief Wizard of Dun Indewood and, along with Humfrey, a partner of *Boggart and Rune – Pryvate Inquestigators* ("crimes solved before they happen") ignored the boggart, but continued to stare at Bertram with a mixture of speculation and apprehension. "Explain thyself!"

Bertram told them what he had learnt from Councillor Shale about his half-human ancestry, and how he had come to leave Caer Borundum. "So you see," he concluded, "they threw me down a waterfall to almost certain death. I decided they were trying to tell me that I wasn't welcome among trolls, so I thought I'd try my luck among humans instead."

"Shtrange shtory." Humfrey scratched his head. "Well, you're here now, sho it looksh like we gotta figure out what to do with you." The boggart turned again to his silent companion. "Hey, Runie. Any ideash?"

The Runemaster slumped back into his chair, staring fixedly at the white, carved runestones. At length he shook his head. "I cannot advise thee. Thou must decide. I have no prediction to make. On this matter, the runes are silent."

Humfrey scowled. "Shome wizard you are, partner!" He regarded the Runemaster doubtfully, then shrugged and turned back to Bertram. "Well, the way I shee it, you haven't done anything wrong. You shay you want to shettle here in Dun Indewood – hey, letsh give it a go! We got weirder thingsh here than trollsh and lemmingsh." At a gesture from the ex-King of Thieves, the Badgers around the room relaxed. Humfrey shot Bertram a shrewd look. "You got anywhere to shtay?"

"To what? Oh, to stay." Bertram blinked. "No. No, we haven't."

"Come on, then." Humfrey picked up his hat. "I know a guy who'sh pretty broad-minded. Pretty broad in all directionsh, if it comesh to that."

Luigi the Pastafarian, all-round chef (quite literally) and owner of the *Pizza Palace and Premier Comfort Lodge Hotel,* eyed Bertram doubtfully. 'Oly cannelloni! You're a big boy of your mamma's, aren't you? Can you cook?"

Bertram gave the roly-poly pasta chef an anxious look. "I can cook rock cakes."

"Pfui!" Luigi puffed his cheeks out. Then he grinned. "I try you out as my delivery boy. One thing fo' sure – nobody gonna try an' mug a pizza delivery guy lookin' like you!"

And so Bertram found himself delivering for Luigi's Pizza Palace. At first, the pastafarian accompanied Bertram on his rounds, nodding his multicoloured dreadlocks in approval as well-known members of Dun Indewood's criminal community were brought up short at the sight of Bertram. The would-be muggers hastily melted away into the crowds that thronged the City's narrow streets and twisting alleys, mentally revising their plans to make an unauthorised cash withdrawal from the Bank of Luigi.

Over the following days, Bertram became a familiar sight on the cobbled streets of Dun Indewood. Having failed to fit on Luigi's gaily painted delivery cart, which had given a tortured groan and threatened to collapse under his weight, Bertram decided that he'd be better off making the deliveries on foot. So he strode along beside the dog cart, while Luigi's canine companion, Hot Dog, pulled it through the narrow streets. Cliff, perched on the driver's seat, encouraged Hot Dog with shrill cries of "Mush!" Hot Dog completely ignored the lemming, but trotted from delivery to delivery with the good-humoured lope of big dogs everywhere, panting and lolling his tongue in the overheated way that had earned him his name.

After the first few days, people stopped staring. The citizens of Dun Indewood were a phlegmatic bunch and, as Humfrey had said, many of the creatures that left the uncertain world of the Dark Forest for the security of Dun Indewood were a lot weirder than trolls. Bertram, to his astonishment, found that he was even becoming popular. True, he couldn't negotiate some of the more rickety stairs or smaller doorways of the City's tumbledown houses, but he always called loudly so customers who lived there could hear him coming, and he always made sure they got their pizzas home safely. This was a considerable bonus for those living in tougher areas of town such as The Grumbles, where it was not unknown for a pizza being carried between cart and front door to be snatched and eaten by neighbours – along with its owner, on occasion.

Bertram had further endeared himself to the citizens of

Dun Indewood by teaching their children a version of the game of trolleyball – though he was forced to substitute an inflated pig's bladder for a proper stone ball after humans proved to be far more breakable than trolls. But the game quickly caught on, and after making his deliveries, Bertram could often be found playing on an improvised court beside Tanner's Trickle (the nearest thing Dun Indewood had to a river). Sensible opponents soon learned not even to try and block Bertram's ferocious and deadly accurate spikes: they simply and wisely stayed out of the way.

Then, one day, something happened to make Bertram's position even more secure.

"Hey! Bertram!" Luigi dusted his podgy hands on his apron and beckoned over his new assistant. "Howzabout you make me some'a those rock cakes you was tellin' me about, hey?" Luigi gave Bertram a hearty pat on the back, stifled a scream and bustled off, wringing his hand.

Bertram's heart sank. Whatever had possessed him to brag to Luigi that he could make rock cakes? He had conveniently omitted the part about trolls finding them inedible. If even trolls hated his rock cakes, how would humans feel about them? But there was no avoiding it – he had to try. He looked around the kitchen anxiously, but there didn't seem to be any grit available. Then Bertram spotted a heap of bags in the corner, filled with the flour that Luigi used to make his pasta and pizza bases. He'd try to use that instead.

When the troll pulled the baking tray from Luigi's oven sometime later, and poked a cake with a huge (and religiously washed) forefinger, he gave a moan of despair. These cakes were even softer and crumblier than the ones he'd made back home in Caer Borundum. Luigi would throw them in his face... tell him he was a fraud... sack him!

At that moment, Luigi bustled back in, accompanied by Humfrey. "Hi, there, tough guy," said the boggart pleasantly. "I jusht came by to shee how you're doin'."

"He's doin' hokay," Luigi reassured him. The pastafarian turned to Bertram. "Hey, big boy! How's those cakes a-comin'?" Luigi eyed the cooling mounds appreciatively. "Mmmm-mmmm! Fresh from the oven. Le's see if you's as good a cook as me!" Laughing uproariously at his own joke, Luigi popped one of Bertram's creations into his mouth. His laughter died instantly.

Bertram shut his eyes. After a while, when nothing happened, he opened them again. Luigi was standing stock-still, his expression perfectly blank, chewing slowly. Bertram shut his eyes again. Then he opened them again. And opened them wider.

A look of dreamy contentment was spreading over Luigi's ample features. His eyes held the look of a pastafarian who had beheld strange wonders. His lips curved in a blissful smile.

Wordlessly, he held out the baking tray to Humfrey, who reached for a cake, sniffed it suspiciously and took a mouthful.

The hard-bitten Private Inquestigator closed his eyes.

"Mmmmmmmmmmmm," he remarked.

"*Mmmmmmmmmmm,*" Luigi explained.

Bertram stared at Humfrey and Luigi in disbelief. "You mean – you like them?"

"Oooooooooooooooo," Humfrey confirmed.

"*Oooooooooooooooo,*" Luigi agreed.

Bertram couldn't believe his ears. "Are you sure? They're not too crumbly?"

"Delishioush."

"Stupendous!"

"Lushioush!"

"Divine! They's as light as a feather!"

"They melt in your mouth," the boggart agreed, reaching for another.

"Hey!" Luigi slapped Humfrey's wrist.

"Awwww!" Humfrey gave Luigi a piteous look. "Can't I have seconds?"

"No!" Luigi snatched the cakes away. "These go on sale in my restaurant. Tonight!"

And to Bertram's astonishment, his rock cakes proved to be a sensation among the clientele of the Pizza Palace. Soon, Bertram was working overtime, Luigi was ordering in extra flour, and the watermill powered by Tanner's Trickle was taking on extra staff and working a shift system to keep up with demand. Dun Indewood's citizens from Knyght to knave were clamouring for the new delicacy. To celebrate the new sensation, Luigi changed his establishment's name to *The Pizza Palace and Patisserie (We're Passionate about Pastry!).*

But there was also a downside to Bertram's new career...

"Come out!" Bertram poked the long handle of the bread-paddle into the furthest recesses of the oven.

"Shan't!" Cliff's voice echoed defiantly from the fire-blackened interior.

"What do you think you're doing in there?"

"Cleaning," lied the lemming.

Bertram sighed. "I wish you'd stop hiding in the ovens. You know I always look inside before I light the fire."

"You might forget," said Cliff in sulky tones.

"I've got a dozen double batches to bake today! Will you come out?"

"No!"

But on the whole, things were going better than Bertram had ever dared hope for. Contrary to his fears, humans weren't evil monsters. True, there were rude humans, deceitful humans, selfish humans – just as there were rude, deceitful and selfish trolls. Generally, Bertram got on well with people. He was happy, he was busy and, for the first time in his life, he felt appreciated. In fact, he was in danger of feeling that he fitted in... even belonged.

So, all in all, it was a bit of a shock when Humfrey turned up very early one morning with a whole company of grim-faced guards at his back and arrested Bertram as a spy.

Chapter Four

How Bertram found himself in a Torturous Situation and a Dark Shadow brought Gloom.

Robat fitzBadly, High Lord of Dun Indewood, limped into the torture chamber of his Castle accompanied by Humfrey and the Runemaster. The low, dark, stone room with its vaulted ceiling was lit only by guttering torches and the deep red glow of a brazier on which branding irons crackled and pinged as they warmed to operating temperature.

Lord Robat leaned on his stick and squinted into the gloom. "Scumbucket!" he bawled.

Roofus Scumbucket, the Official Torturer to the High Lords, shuffled forwards in a respectful cringe.

Lord Robat waved his stick at Bertram, who was chained

to a stone pillar in the centre of the dungeon. "Well?" he demanded in a high, reedy voice. "Has the creature been persuaded to talk?"

Roofus Scumbucket was not a happy man. Since the demise of Lord Gordin, the previous ruler of the City, there had been no call for his particular and peculiar services. Lord Robat had been persuaded (somewhat reluctantly) by the Runemaster that there were more civilised ways to extract information from prisoners. Forced into semi-retirement, Roofus had been given a job in the tax office, where he felt right at home asking lots of awkward questions – though to his disappointment, he was not allowed to subject people who told him fibs to unspeakable torments.

This situation had suddenly changed a few hours previously, when Roofus had been woken in the middle of the night by several armed guards banging on the rickety door of his house in The Grumbles to inform him that Lord Robat required his services at the Castle. Pulling on his moth-eaten regulation black leather jerkin and trousers, and retrieving his executioner's hood from the cat basket, the semi-retired torturer had been frogmarched to the Castle to reacquaint himself with the tools of his profession. On seeing his 'client', Roofus Scumbucket had suddenly begun to wish that he'd made his retirement permanent.

The torturer shook his head. "Er, well, your guv'norships, in a word and not to beat about the bush whilst getting straight to the point and in a manner of speakin'..." He shook his head miserably. "No. He's not said a thing."

Behind him, chains rattled. Bertram gave his captors a stony stare. Humfrey shook his head angrily. "I told you, Your Highnesh, thish ishn't the way to..."

"Silence!" Lord Robat glowered at his Chief Inquestigator. "Do I need to remind you, Master Boggart, who it was allowed this spy to come among us in the first place?"

"Who says I'm a spy?" demanded Bertram furiously.

"He isn't!" a shrill voice piped up. Lord Robat looked down in astonishment at the small rodent who was tugging at the hem of his cloak. "He's not a spy," Cliff repeated, "but I am. You should put an end to me, you really should!"

Lord Robat stared. "What is this vermin doing here?"

Cliff stamped his paw. "Who are you calling vermin? I insisted on accompanying the prisoner! I am his legal adviser and..."

"Thish ish ridiculoush," interrupted Humfrey. He pointed at Scumbucket. "I wouldn't trusht thish guy to get information out of an encyclopaedia."

Roofus bristled. Things weren't going well, but a torturer has his pride. "Listen, small stuff..."

The boggart looked daggers at Roofus. "Can it, wise guy. I ain't forgotten how you treated me an' Luigi when we ended up in your dungeon, sho you ain't getting no teshtimonial from me anywaysh. Are you telling ush the troll hashn't shpilled the beansh?"

Roofus wrung his hands. "No, he hasn't – but it wasn't my fault!" he wailed.

Lord Robat lost his temper. "What do I pay you for?" he

stormed at the unhappy torturer. "I gave you an express order to take the troll to the dungeon and find out whether he was a spy!"

Roofus held out his hands imploringly. "Well, guv'nor – that was the beginnin' of the problem. We couldn't actually get him into the dungeon – he's too big. We 'ad to knock an extra door through." He pointed to a pile of stone against the far wall. Beyond it, a chill draught moaned through an irregular, troll-sized hole.

Humfrey grinned at the torturer. "Look on the bright shide. You've probably got the only dungeon in the Foresht with a patio door." Roofus stifled a sob.

Lord Robat gave an exasperated sigh. "All right – but you got him down here eventually. I suppose you have tortured him?"

"I tried!" Roofus's voice was a howl. "I really did! I went through my whole repertoire. No good – any of it."

Lord Robat pursed his lips. "Did you try the thumbscrews?"

Roofus nodded miserably.

"They wouldn't go round my thumbs," interjected Bertram helpfully.

Lord Robat glared at his captive. "What about the rack?"

Roofus indicated a pile of splintered wood in the corner. "Ruined! He lay on it and it smashed to bits!" He gave a small sob. "And it was a family heirloom. My grandaddy left it to me on 'is deathbed – come to think of it, it *was* 'is deathbed..."

Bertram looked embarrassed. "Sorry."

Lord Robat ground his teeth. "Did you try *everything*? The Iron Maiden?"

"Couldn't get him in – the doors wouldn't shut."

"The boot?"

"Too small. I tried that on his thumbs, but the sharp pointy bits bent on his skin."

"The red-hot pokers?"

"They tickled," Bertram complained.

In the ensuing silence, the Runemaster crossed the stone floor to stand before Bertram. For the first time since entering the dungeon, he spoke. "Why dost thou refuse to answer our questions?"

Bertram looked puzzled. "No one's asked me any questions. What do you want to know?"

Roofus Scumbucket felt himself turning red as all eyes in the room fixed on him. Lord Robat gave him a menacing look. "Scumbucket! Did you actually ask the troll any questions?" Roofus stared at the High Lord and shook his head. Lord Robat raised his eyes to the stone ceiling. "Why not?"

"Protocol, Your Guv'norship." Roofus was scandalised. "Everythin' in its proper order. Torturin' first *then* questions! Going straight to questions ain't right. It's not in the true order of things! Why," protested the torturer indignantly, "if you was to go rushin' straight to questions, without the torturin', there wouldn't be any need for me!"

Humfrey cleared his throat in a meaningful sort of way. Lord Robat gave the boggart a resigned nod. "Very well, Master Humfrey. We'll try it your way."

Half an hour later, Bertram was standing on top of the ancient tower of the Citadel.

This was the highest part of the Castle, the fortress of the ancient kings of Dun Indewood whose line had died out many years before. Long a ruin, the Citadel was being restored on the orders of the Runemaster. Wooden scaffolding clung to its ragged walls, and piles of dressed stone lay dotted about waiting to be cemented into position.

Cliff perched on the battlements and gazed at the dizzying drop to the cobbled courtyard below. "Whooo," he said dreamily, "what a long way down." Wordlessly, Bertram snatched the lemming and stuffed him headfirst into a fold of his jerkin.

The night was almost done. There was a faint tinge of pink in the sky to the east. By its light, Bertram could see the Runemaster, Humfrey and the guards who had brought him to this vantage point. Lord Robat, muttering about his gout, had baulked at the stiff climb and remained in his apartments with orders that the troll's confession should be brought to him by breakfast time.

The Runemaster bowed to Bertram.

"On the High Lord's behalf," he said solemnly, "I apologise for thy unkind treatment: but these are anxious times and worried men may forget the courtesy due to guests and strangers."

Nonplussed, but wishing to be polite, Bertram nodded.

"The question we would have thee answer is simple." The Runemaster looked Bertram straight in the eye. "Since thou camest to this City, hast thou had any contact with thy people?"

Bertram shook his head. "No. Not since I left Caer Borundum."

The Runemaster held Bertram's glance for some moments, then nodded slowly. "I believe thee," he said. "Moreover, the runes indicate that thou speakest true."

Humfrey rubbed his chin. "Are you shure we can trusht thish guy?"

"I'm telling the truth!" Bertram protested. "Anyway, what makes you think I've been in contact with the trolls?"

The Runemaster took a deep breath. "For many days now, every casting of the runes has foreshadowed peril and disaster. In all my years of prediction and divination, never have I seen such a grave configuration of the stones. All is darkness. Every time I recast, the stones fall exactly as before. Then last night, whilst I pondered on their message, we received disturbing reports from afar, brought to us by our City messenger, Whizzard Tym—"

Before the Runemaster could finish speaking, a sallow-faced youth suddenly appeared out of thin air. "My ears are burning. Did somebody call?"

Humfrey greeted the new arrival with a wink and a nod. "Hi, Whizzshkid. Shtill lishtening at keyholesh? Nice entranshe."

Bertram blinked in disbelief. "Where did he spring from?" he demanded.

The new arrival grinned. "Sorry if I scared you. Didn't the Runemaster tell you? I'm a Whizzard – I can travel faster than the eye can see."

Bertram blinked. "That must be very useful."

"He is our messenger," said the Runemaster, "bringing us news from the far reaches of the Dark Forest and beyond." He turned to Tym. "Recount the news thou brought to me last night."

Tym gave Bertram an uncertain glance. "Here? Now?" The Runemaster nodded and the boy shrugged. "Oh, well. On my recent travels, I visited Gnomansland, the capital city of the gnomes, to see my old friend Prince Feobald." Bertram was surprised. Gnomes were reclusive creatures. He was amazed to find that they had any friends – especially among humans.

Tym continued, "He gave me news that has been concerning the gnomes, dwarves and other peoples of the underworld. Rumours are flying around that the trolls have discovered the lost Hall of the Mountain King and, within it, the Obsidian Throne."

Bertram gave a gasp. "The Throne! But that's just a legend."

"Many legends have substance." The Runemaster gestured to Tym. "Continue."

"This discovery has been used by the Troll Lord..."

"What Troll Lord?" exclaimed Bertram, "We don't have a Troll Lord. Or a king, or anything like that. We have the Trollmoot and councillors..."

Humfrey raised an eyebrow. "We?"

"I mean trolls..." Bertram fell silent.

"It seems that things have changed greatly since thou left Caer Borundum," said the Runemaster drily. He turned to Tym. "Finish thy report."

Tym nodded. "Whether it's true about the Throne or not, the trolls are certainly on the warpath. They started with raids on the gobblings – not that anyone cares what happens to *them*." The young Whizzard gave an involuntary shudder as he remembered the time he was attacked by the pint-sized predators. "But the trolls have been going after the gnomes too – driving them out of their caverns and taking prisoners to work in the mines."

Bertram gaped at the messenger. "That can't be! Trolls are peaceable."

Tym shook his head. "Not any more, apparently. According to Feobald, a whole army of them is marching down out of the mountains, all kitted out with heavy clubs, big rocks and bad attitudes. And they're heading this way."

Bertram shook his head in bewilderment. "There must be some mistake."

"No mistake," said Tym firmly. "I saw the army myself, on the way back here."

The Runemaster nodded. "Thou knowest thy mission, Master Whizzard. Be thou about it straight." Tym bowed to the old wizard, grinned at Bertram and winked at Humfrey – and was gone in the blink of an eye.

The Runemaster took up the story. "With the discovery of the Obsidian Throne, their new Lord hath incited the trolls to rise up. The Troll Lord hath sworn vengeance and promised to claim back all that, in his view, rightfully belongs to the troll people. He hath assembled an army of warriors and sent them out to wreak havoc on their ancient enemies."

"In other wordsh, humansh," said Humfrey.

Bertram shook his head in bewilderment. "But even if what you say is true, and there is a troll army – why would it come here?"

The Runemaster's eyes glinted in the first rays of the rising sun. "Because Dun Indewood is built on the site of the destroyed troll city."

Bertram felt as though the solid stone tower was reeling beneath his feet. "You mean – this is where Trollingrad used to be?"

The Runemaster nodded. "When it was captured at the end of the Troll-Man Wars many years ago, the troll city was demolished and Dun Indewood rose in its place. Only the innermost defensive work of the trolls was spared and reused as the heart of the human fortification." The old man gave a wry smile. "Thou art standing on it."

Bertram shakily ran his fingers over the rough stone of the battlements. "Then the Citadel...?"

"Is all that remains of Trollingrad." The Runemaster nodded. "But now, it seems, the trolls wish to retake their seat of power and restore their rule over the outer world."

"Sho it sheems a bit of a coinshidensh," said Humfrey in a voice laden with irony, "that jusht before thish troll army marchesh out, a troll, i.e. you, turnsh up here in Dun Indewood. Shome people – Lord Robat for inshtance – think that makesh you a shpy!"

Bertram stared at the Boggart, aghast. "I'm not a shpy! I mean, a spy!"

Humfrey gave Bertram a narrow-eyed stare. "No? You're telling ush you didn't know any of thish?"

To his horror, Bertram suddenly recalled the conversation he'd heard at the falls between Granite and the stranger in the shadows. They had talked of revenge and doom...

"No," he replied, a little too quickly.

Humfrey said nothing, but kept his eyes on the troll. His expression was implacable.

"Thou mayst not be a spy, but thou *art* half a troll." The Runemaster's voice was low and troubled. "Bertram, we would not willingly lay this doom upon thee. But events force our hand. Thou must choose. Wilt thou help the trolls to take Dun Indewood and destroy it? Or wilt thou help us to defend the City against the troll army?"

Head bowed, Bertram wandered away from Humfrey and the Runemaster and sat with his back to a turret. Humfrey made as if to follow his, but was stopped by the Runemaster. Boggart and wizard conversed in heated whispers.

Bertram took Cliff from his jerkin pocket and set the lemming down on his knee. "What do you think I should do?" he asked helplessly. "If I help the humans to save their City, I'll be betraying the trolls: my own people. Councillor Shale, Opal – even my mother!"

Cliff gave him a hard stare. "But the trolls threw you out, remember? And if you don't help the humans, it'll be 'goodbye, Dun Indewood'! And what happens then to all the people who've been kind to us?"

"I know!" Bertram felt as if his head was about to explode. "I've got to choose one side or the other, and I'll betray half my heritage whatever side I choose."

"Then you'd better choose the right side," said Cliff tartly.

"But which is the right side? The humans put the trolls under the Man-curse and that was wrong..."

"True," said Cliff, "but maybe it was their only hope. Trolls are a lot bigger and stronger than humans. Anyway, all that happened long ago."

Bertram nodded slowly. "You're right. The only thing we know for sure is that the people who live in Dun Indewood *now* are in danger, although they haven't done anything to threaten the trolls. Here and now, my people are the aggressors."

Bertram stood up and went back to the Runemaster. "I will help you to keep the troll army at bay." He shrugged. "If I can."

The Runemaster gave him a nod and the briefest flicker of a smile. Humfrey looked thoughtful, but nodded slowly.

"Hang on a minute!" Cliff had followed Bertram and was now dancing excitedly around his feet. "We're talking about trolls, right? How can a troll army march above ground? Even in the Forest, there wouldn't be complete shade. As soon as the sun rose, the entire army would turn to stone!" Bertram nodded dumbly – why hadn't he thought of that?

"Yep – that had ush wondering too." Humfrey's voice was as laconic as ever, but the tension in it was unmistakable. "That'sh why we brought you guysh up here. Take a look to the north."

"The north?" Puzzled, Bertram turned northwards – and felt his heart miss a beat. Shock burst ice-cold within him like a sword-thrust in the vitals. Numbly, he stared at the impossible.

The sun had risen and was now a blinding red disc on the eastern horizon, its light washing the ancient stones of the Citadel the colour of blood. The sky around it was a blaze of bronze and gold. But in the north, a creeping darkness was spreading over the endless trees of the Forest. No longer hidden by night, the blackness crawled across the landscape like the shadow of a stormcloud. But there were no clouds. And the shadow seemed to come, not from the sky, but from the earth itself.

Bertram remembered the slates Councillor Shale had shown him. The beautiful jewels, the fine metalwork... He'd thought they were just legends. But if the Throne and the Hall had been discovered, perhaps the legendary weapons of the trolls weren't legends after all. Bertram recalled the councillor's words: *"The power of the Sceptre was this: it could drain the light of the sun from the sky. The Sceptre cast a shadow over the troll host, so that it could attack the humans even during the hours of daylight..."*

Cliff stared at the approaching shadow and shivered. "I have a bad feeling about this. And when a *lemming* gets a bad feeling..." He fell silent.

The Runemaster moved to stand beside Bertram. "Dost thou know what this means?"

"Yes," Bertram replied tonelessly. "It means that the trolls have found more than the Hall and the Throne. They have found one of their ultimate weapons against the power of man. They have found the Sceptre of the Last Stygian Kings."

The Runemaster nodded as if his worst fears had been realised. "Then the reports are true. The troll host will soon be upon us."

The party gathered on the tower of the Citadel watched in silence as the shadow moved closer: on and inexorably on. They gazed out over the Dark Forest as treetop after treetop was engulfed behind a veil of despair; a cloak of death; a dark and bitter shroud of doom.

Chapter Five

How the Gloom Deepened and Dun Indewood found itself Entirely Surrounded by Trolls.

The armoury was full of lords, Knyghts, guard commanders and other officials, all waving maps and diagrams about and shouting at the tops of their voices. On Lord Robat's orders, Humfrey had called them together to plan the defence of the city against the approaching troll army.

There were varying opinions. People who wanted to build defensive walls were engaged in bitter arguments with people who wanted to dig defensive ditches in exactly the same place. Because of his knowledge of trolls, Bertram had been appointed unofficial adviser to the planners; but because he was unofficial (and a troll) nobody was listening to him.

A very tall, thin figure with a monocle, a beaky nose and no chin hammered on the table with his steel gauntlet until his ill-fitting armour rattled. Sir Ronild the Reckless had the reputation of being the bravest Knyght in Dun Indewood. It was said that he had once challenged a goat that was eating his begonias to single combat and had very nearly put it to flight.

"The Knyghts of Dun Indewood," declaimed Sir Ronild, "shall not be found wanting! We shall stand firm against the troll menace!" The other Knyghts coughed warningly and shuffled their feet. This sounded like fighting talk to them and they didn't like it one bit.

"We shall ride out upon the foe," continued Sir Ronild, going purple with excitement, "shoulder to shoulder, our lances in our hands, and meet them with charge after glorious charge—"

"Until you've all been smashed to smithereens," interrupted Bertram wearily. All eyes in the room turned to him. "Have you ever tried charging a troll with a wooden lance?"

Sir Ronild lowered his eyes and shook his head.

"I wouldn't advise it," said Bertram kindly. "It would be like attacking a wall of solid rock armed with a stick of celery. Sheer suicide."

Cliff waved a tiny paw. "I would like to volunteer—"

Bertram 'accidentally' nudged Cliff off the table.

Sir Ronild's face was a picture of misery. "So what sort of weapon might work against trolls?"

"Hammers," said Bertram. "You need to arm yourself with a big..." He broke off as he took in the Knyght's spindly arms and woebegone expression. "That is, a medium-sized... a *small* hammer. Or a pick." (Bertram had discovered that humans made substitute picksies out of metal.) "And be ready to swing it really, really hard."

Sir Ronild eyed Bertram dubiously. "So if we armed ourselves with hammers, we could prevail against the trolls?"

A troll, Bertram thought, nodding in an encouraging way. If there were a lot of you, and if it was a very small troll. A very small, *weak* troll. But he didn't say this out loud. Sir Ronild went off, shaking his head unhappily. An explosion of noise erupted as the planners continued their arguments.

Unable to take the chaos any longer, Humfrey the Boggart made his way through the crowd by the simple method of elbowing anyone who was in his way viciously in the kneecaps, leaving a trail of writhing officials in his wake. He leapt on to a table, put a finger and thumb to his mouth and gave a strident whistle.

"Shilence!"

Hush fell. The people nearest Humfrey gave him reproving looks and wiped saliva off their plans. Humfrey affected not to notice this and turned to Bertram. "Whaddaya shay, big guy? Wallsh or ditchesh?"

"Ditches," said Bertram instantly. "Deep ones. Filled with water. Trolls can smash through stone walls in seconds, but they don't like water. And they're too heavy to swim well."

Humfrey turned back to the crowd of officials. "You heard the big feller. Ditchesh it ish. Now get goin'!"

Gathering their plans and their dignity the officials stalked out, casting resentful glances at Bertram as they went.

Humfrey snorted. "Expertsh! They'd shtill be arguing when the troll army getsh here." He shook his head. "It'sh a good thing we've got people round here who jusht get on with the tashk in hand. What shay you an' me take a look at the preparashionsh?"

Bertram looked momentarily nonplussed. "Preparashionsh?"

"Shure. Of the defenshesh."

Bertram clicked his fingers. The weapons on the walls rattled. "Oh – the preparations of the defences!"

"That'sh eashy for you to shay."

They began in the Castle courtyard, where the Citizens' Militia was being drilled. A motley company of tradesmen, merchants and shopkeepers were stumbling about, trying to keep in step with each other and hopping desperately when they fell out of it. They carried a bizarre collection of weapons – farmers brandished pitchforks, woodsmen axes, blacksmiths hammers. A barber was marching with a pair of curling tongs. Bertram considered asking him what he thought he was going to do with them, but on reflection decided that he really didn't want to know. He saw Luigi trying to shoulder arms with his bread-paddle and winced. This ragged band would be lucky to last five minutes against the trolls.

On the City walls, he and Humfrey met the ex-King of Thieves patrolling with a company of bowmen. They at least seemed to know what they were doing. The ex-King gave Humfrey a casual salute.

"Nuffin' much to report," he said. "We sent Big Jim an' some of the lads up north on a recce mission. They're in the Forest harryin' the trolls. Well, I *say* harryin' – it's no use shootin' arrows at trolls, they just bounce off. We've caught a few in pits and bear traps – that won't stop 'em, o' course, but it slows 'em up a bit."

Descending from the Castle, Bertram and Humfrey paused to watch a ragged figure rowing a dilapidated boat up and down the Trickle between the Upper Water Gate and the Tavern Bridge. The movement of the boat was a bit haphazard as the rower kept using his one good hand to raise a brown bottle to his lips. In the intervals between swigs he sang rude songs about mermaids or yelled incomprehensible nautical oaths at nobody in particular.

Humfrey sighed. "That'sh Captain Gorge. We've made him Admiral of the Fleet."

Bertram stared at the boggart. "But we haven't got a fleet."

"No, but it keepsh him happy and out of the way."

Their next port of call was the Main Gate. Word had quickly spread throughout the Forest of the advancing troll army and a stream of refugees from outlying villages and farmsteads was heading to the relative safety of Dun Indewood.

The Main Gate was closed: only the small postern door let into one side was open. Rolph, the guard in charge of the gate, had set up a rickety desk beside it. The desk was covered in forms. Rolph had one of these laid out before him. He was writing on it very slowly with a stub of pencil (which he kept pausing to lick) as he interviewed a stolid-looking forester.

"Now then," said Rolph placidly. "Question forty-seven. Are you: a) seeking to escape from a combat zone; b) fleeing political or religious persecution; or c) an economic migrant?"

The forester stared at Rolph. "What?"

Rolph put the form down and fixed the forester with a steady look. "Why do you want to come in?"

The forester placed his knuckles on the desk and leaned forward until he and the guard were practically eyeball-to-eyeball. "Because," he said in measured, emphatic tones, "I don't want some dirty big troll ripping my head off and playing football with it!"

Rolph nodded serenely and licked his pencil. "I'll put that down as fleeing political or religious persecution... Next!"

"I claig political ashylum," said a voice Bertram recognised. The troll's eyes widened. The creature standing in front of Rolph was wearing a peasant's hood, but the nose that poked out of it was suspiciously long, grey and hairy, and most definitely belonging to the Highwaywolf. "Ang gy the way, can oo direck gee koo a goog denkist?"

Humfrey sighed as he led Bertram away. "Lord Robat'sh orders," he told the bewildered troll. "All ashylum sheekersh musht make an application for reshidence in Dun Indewood which musht then be processhed..."

"But that'll take ages!" protested Bertram. "The shadow

is getting closer and closer. According to the reconnaissance patrols, the Troll Lord's army is not far behind. When it gets here, most of those people will still be outside. They'll be massacred."

"I don't think sho," said Humfrey calmly. "Ash shoon ash it'sh dark, Rolph opensh the gatesh quietly and letsh them all in."

Bertram shook his head. "That's crazy."

Humfrey shrugged. "That'sh the way it goesh in Dun Indewood. We do thingsh by the book until it getsh too dark to read: then we throw the book away and do whatever worksh."

Bertram pondered this as they moved on through the City.

A few days later, Bertram stood with Cliff, Humfrey, the Runemaster and Lord Robat and his commanders on the battlements above the North Gate.

The shadow created by the Sceptre of the Troll Kings lay heavily over Dun Indewood. There was no day: only a murky, dull twilight. The shadow was not simply a barrier to the sun, such as might be caused by a dark cloud or an eclipse. It drifted through the hushed streets like a dense, suffocating blanket of fog, deadening footfalls and leaching hope from the hearts of the inhabitants. If they had to go out, City dwellers scuttled furtively from place to place, their cloaks wrapped tightly round their bodies, their shoulders hunched. Those with no business outdoors banked their fires against the chill and huddled together for warmth and comfort.

The surrounding countryside was deserted. The last of the Badgers, weary, footsore and out of arrows, had limped in some time ago. The villagers and woodsmen had already sought refuge in the city. Displaced families huddled in stables and doorways. Their animals roamed the streets, grunting, bleating and lowing in unhappy confusion.

The troll army had begun to arrive several hours before. All through the long, dull day, trolls had poured out of the Dark Forest. Companies of troll engineers had cleared a space for the vast encampment by the simple expedient of tearing down the ancient trees with their bare hands. After this, armed with picksies and iron axes, they had hacked and shaped the fallen trunks into weapons of war – ballistas, trebuchets, siege bows and battering rams. The smaller branches they had simply gathered into huge piles and set alight. The regiments of troll infantry had gathered round these, shouting and singing. Trolls were not keen on sunlight, but they did like warmth.

Now, the troll companies covered the entire plain between the City walls and the Forest, from the jousting field to the Upper Water Gate. Acrid smoke rose from their fires, and from the hamlets and homesteads they had burnt on the way, and rolled over the walls of Dun Indewood in choking clouds. To the south-west, the ruins of the village of Swains Willingly smouldered, while trolls cut lumbering capers among the debris, shouting threats and insults.

Lord Robat broke the gloomy silence. "I say," he muttered, "there's an awful lot of the bounders, what?"

"Would you like me to challenge the whole army to single combat?" asked Cliff brightly. "Just say the word."

Bertram quelled the lemming with a look. "Every male troll in Caer Borundum seems to be here," he said unhappily, staring out over the ever-increasing host. "The city must be half-deserted."

"It sheemsh to me," said Humfrey grimly, "that the shituashion hash become shomewhat sherioush."

Lord Robat wiped his hand across his cloak. "Master Boggart, you will oblige me by refraining from statements of the obvious. Especially when you half drown me while making them." The ruler of Dun Indewood gazed out over the troll army and shook his head sorrowfully. "We can do nothing against numbers such as these."

The Runemaster nodded in gloomy agreement. "All our preparations have miscarried. Too late, I learnt from friend Bertram of the nature of the enemy's weapon of darkness. Had we known of the Sceptre in time, we could have sent Whizzard Tym to steal it from their innermost treasury. But I had already sent him to the dragons of the Dark Forest in the hope that their flames might drive back the darkness of the trolls' weapon. There is none swift enough to recall him. And I doubt that even the dragons' aid – should they agree to offer it – will be sufficient to overcome such a host."

Humfrey pointed. "It looksh like the trollsh are shending an embasshy."

The others gazed in the direction of his pointing finger. Humfrey was right. Outside an elaborate golden pavilion that had taken a company of engineers several hours to erect, a column of trolls, grimly imposing in their iron battle armour, was forming up. Flags and pennants were being hoisted. Eventually, to the muffled beat of moleskin drums, the company set off, approaching the gate of the City. At its centre rumbled a huge chariot pulled by four great war-moles richly caparisoned in sable, deep gold and blood red. On the cart stood an elaborate throne, upon which lounged a figure clad in golden armour.

The Runemaster looked thoughtful. "That does not look like a herald."

Humfrey shook his head. "From the way he'sh lazing about while the othersh are doing all the work, I'd shay he'sh their leader."

Bertram said nothing but stared at the approaching figure.

The cart halted just beyond the first hastily dug defensive ditch, almost within bow-shot of the gate. Its occupant struggled to his feet and gazed up at the defenders watching from the gatehouse. He cupped his hands round his mouth, and cried:

"Listen up! I am..."

His voice was drowned by a blare of trumpets and trollbones as his escort blew a fanfare in his honour. The troll in the golden armour turned round and berated his men. Though the music drowned out his voice, the gestures were unmistakable – especially when he began throwing things at the players. As the music petered out in a series of sad little off-key blats and parps, the troll leader, still glowering, turned his attention back on his foes.

"Yeah, right, like I was sayin' – you listen to me – right? The Troll Lord made me general o' this army, so what I say goes, right? The Troll Lord, he says you got..." The leader paused and started to count on his fingers. His lips were visibly moving. "Twenty-four hours! You got twenty-four hours to surren... surrin..." He paused again, his lips moving frantically. "To give up! See? An' if you sarrun... serram... dat fing, we let you go free an' just take der City."

The Runemaster stepped forward. "And if we refuse to surrender," he cried. "How then?"

For a moment the troll leader looked nonplussed. An aide hurriedly clambered on to the cart and whispered something into his ear. They heard the leader snap, "Yeah, right! I knew dat!" When he raised his head again, there was an ugly grin plastered across his brutal features.

"Den we come in," he boomed happily, "an' smash you up good!"

Lord Robat raised his voice. "We will take counsel, and let you know our decision."

The troll leader gave him a baffled look. "Wha'?"

Humfrey rolled his eyes. "He shaid we'll think about it!"

"Yeah, well..." The troll leader pointed a finger like a gatepost at the defenders. "Don't fink too long!" The troll struck a warlike pose, which was slightly spoilt when, a few moments later, the chariot jerked into motion and sent him sprawling back on his throne. The escort wheeled about, heading back to camp.

The Runemaster gave a grim smile. "So there we have it. Not what I'd call a diplomatic speech, but the meaning was clear enough. I wonder why they want our surrender?"

Humfrey nodded agreement. "They can jusht roll ush over any time they like. Maybe they want to avoid casualtiesh."

"Or perhaps," said Lord Robat, "they simply want to humiliate us."

"Could be." Humfrey turned to Bertram. "What did our reshident troll make of all that?"

But Bertram said nothing. He was staring after the departing troll leader, open-mouthed. His fingers were gripping the battlements so hard the stone was crumbling.

Humfrey clicked his fingers. "Hey! Big guy! Shnap out of it! What'sh eating you?" His eyes narrowed shrewdly. "You know that guy?"

Bertram turned shocked eyes on the boggart. "Know him? I'll say I know him! That's the troll who threw me over the falls. That's the troll I heard plotting against humans. That's Granite Moraine!"

Chapter Six

Of Cunning Plans and Artful Disguises, and why you should Never send a Lemming to do a Troll's Job.

"Have you seen the size of them! Dam' great big things!"

"Someone should do something about it!"

"Monstrous! Shouldn't be allowed!"

"I've half a mind to write to someone."

"Yes, I've half a mind as well!"

The Great Hall of Dun Indewood gleamed with the flickering light of hundreds of candles. Their glow failed to dispel the atmosphere of gloom caused by the shadow of despair beyond the Castle walls.

Following Granite Moraine's ultimatum, an Extraordinary

and Urgent Meeting of the Great Council of the City had been called. Dun Indewood's lords, Knyghts and councillors were arguing over the trolls' demands. Lord Robat tapped his stick fretfully upon the stone dais in a forlorn attempt to bring order to the babble of worried and frightened voices.

Bertram had hurriedly told both the High Lord and the Runemaster all he knew about Granite Moraine. Now the young troll was standing next to the Runemaster, Humfrey and Luigi (who had been promoted Commander of the volunteer City Militia because nobody else wanted the job) in the gallery that ran along the length of the hall. All three gazed glumly down at the chaotic scene.

Bertram was still trying to take in the fact that the Troll Lord – whoever he was – had made Granite the general of his army.

"He's certainly thuggish and brutal enough," he said to Cliff under cover of the din, "but supposing he has to think for himself?"

"Dangerous thing, that," Cliff replied. "When generals start thinking for themselves, one of the first things they think is, 'What am I doing out here with the army, getting cold and being shot at, when I could be warm and safe in the palace giving the orders?' That's how revolutions start. If I was the Troll Lord, the last thing I'd want'd be a general who could think for himself..."

But another thought had occurred to Bertram. "The mysterious voice I heard at the Trollenbach Falls – I wonder if that was the Troll Lord?"

"A decision must be made!" Lord Robat's voice rang out

across the hall, interrupting Bertram's train of thought. The babble dropped to a low muttering. "To recap our predicament, outside the walls is a vast army of trolls, hell-bent on revenge, who wish to take over our City and claim back what they say is theirs. Our assets: the City walls, water-filled ditches, and a few hundred Knyghts, assorted guards and reluctant volunteer groups." This comment was greeted by sheepish looks and the shuffling of feet. "The enemy's assets: size, strength, powerful weapons and overwhelming numbers. Have I missed anything out?"

"You missed out the Parachute Brigade!" piped up a shrill voice. "Which will leap upon our enemies from above! I won't even insist on a parachute!" Cliff's voice was muffled as Bertram hurriedly stuffed the lemming into his pocket.

Sir Ronild the Reckless stood, his nostrils flaring. "Are we cowards?" he demanded. "Let us not despair! Our hearts are strong, our souls are pure..."

"...and our bodies are outnumbered fourteen to one!" Sir Regynild le Bêtenoire, Headmaster of Dun Indewood's Knyght School, shot to his feet. "We can fulminate against these foul, filthy, feculent trolls until we're blue in the backside – but the fact is that the stinking, shifty, subterranean savages have the upper hand! At this moment of desperate and deadly danger, let us say with the prudent, perspicacious, politic and peerless Knyght, Sir Spineless the Yellow: 'He who flees and runs away, lives to flee another day'!"

There was a roar of approval from the gathered Knyghts (nearly all of whom had spent the previous night forging notes saying they had athlete's foot or verrucas, and were excused fighting trolls) except for Sir Ronild, who chewed his moustache and looked mutinous.

Lord Robat gazed at the cheering crowd. "Then that is the decision," he said heavily. "To save our lives, we must accede to our enemies' demands. I will give orders for our peoples to make preparations. They should gather as many possessions as they can carry and prepare to give over Dun Indewood to the trolls."

A roar of agreement swept the hall. Up on the gallery, Humfrey gave a grimace of disapproval. Turning to Bertram and the others, he jerked his thumb towards a door set in the wall behind them. It led to a small private chamber. Here, Luigi and the Runemaster slumped dejectedly in their seats, while Humfrey, scowling furiously, paced up and down. Abruptly, the boggart halted and faced the others squarely.

"Bad decishion," he snapped. "They'll regret it. Maybe not today, maybe not tomorrow, but shoon and for the resht of their livesh."

"Which will probably be quite short," sighed Bertram. "I know Granite. He won't keep his word."

"An' another thing – where we gonna go?" protested Luigi. "We go out there into the Forest, we gonna get eaten by all kindsa scary things, not to mention when the trolls come after us – they turn us into instant bolognese!" The Commander of the City Militia wiped his nose on his apron.

"The point ish thish." Humfrey thrust his chin out. "We can't rely on those lily-livered nincompoopsh in there." He cast a scornful glance at the door from behind which the council proceedings could still be heard. "We have to do shomething decishive and we have to do it shoon."

"Maybe the Runemaster's got somethin' up his sleeve," said Luigi, with a hopeful glance at the old wizard. The Runemaster, making no reply, just stared at the floor.

Humfrey gave a grunt of disgust. "The only thing he'sh got up his shleeve ish an arm and a well-used handkerchief." He looked pointedly at Bertram. "Ever shince you arrived he'sh been ash usheful ash a shuit of marzipan armour. I don't know whatsh wrong with him, but we're going to have to short thish out ourshelvesh."

With a slight movement of air and a deferential cough, the ex-King of Thieves suddenly appeared at Humfrey's elbow with a small, scruffy-looking boy at his side. Luigi gave a start. "Hey! I never heard you come in."

The ex-King of Thieves gave a shamefaced grin. "Sorry. Force of 'abit."

He nodded at his small companion. "This is my nipper. Colyn, say 'ello to the gennlemen."

Colyn gave Bertram a cheeky grin – then howled with pain and started to dance about, waving one hand violently in the air. Attached to it was Cliff, his teeth firmly buried in Colyn's finger.

"Aaghhh! Getitoff! Getitoff!"

The ex-King of Thieves gave a howl of laughter. "That'll teach yer, yer scallywag. Trying to pick Mr Bertram's pockets like that! He takes after 'is old man," explained the reformed thief proudly. "We calls 'im Cutpurse Colyn: best pickpocket in Dun Indewood – apart from yours truly, of course, before I seen the error of my ways." He turned to the leaping Colyn. "Will you stop playing wiv that lemmin' – you'll frighten it to death."

Cliff loosened his grip on Colyn's finger and dropped on to the table. "I should be so lucky," he muttered acidly.

Colyn sucked frantically on his lacerated finger and glared at Bertram. "Pockets big as perishin' saddlebags, an' I choose the one with a livin' burglar alarm."

Humfrey explained the unfortunate turn of events. "It seems to me," said the ex-King of Thieves, "that the nub o' the problem is this Sceptre fing that's stopping the trolls gettin' turned into stone."

Humfrey and Bertram nodded.

"There's your answer. Get rid of this 'ere Sceptre an' the trolls'll have to go back underground or else – instant statchers!"

"'E means statues," Luigi explained to Bertram.

"Thatsh my reading of the situashion," agreed Humfrey. "Thatsh why I ashked you here – any ideash?"

"That's easy," piped up Colyn. "Someone'll 'ave ter nick it."

The boggart's gaze was intense. "Think it can be done?"

"Hmmm, tricky," mused the ex-King of Thieves. "For starters, you'd have ter get out of the city, avoidin' any troll patrols that might be watchin' the gates. Then sneak into their camp an' play 'unt the thimble for this Sceptre item – and when yer do find it, it'll be heavily guarded. Then all you got to do is pinch it an' have it away on yer toes before the trolls twig yer've been. *An'* before Lord Robat surrenders."

"'Oly mascarpone!" exclaimed Luigi. "Tha' sounds like certain death."

Cliff perked up, paw waving frantically in the air. "I'll go! I'll go!"

The ex-King of Thieves shook his head. "This needs to be an inside job."

Humfrey gave a knowing nod. "Sho we need an inshider." Bertram felt all eyes in the room turn to him. "Shomeone who looksh like a troll..." Humfrey went on pointedly. "Or who *ish* a troll..."

Bertram gave a resigned sigh. "All right, all right. What do you want me to do?"

Several hours later, two large shapes crept out from the City's North Gate, both shrouded in long, dark cloaks. One of the figures marched determinedly towards the troll camp. The other figure was less purposeful, staggering and lurching from side to side across the furrowed earth.

"Left... right... straighten up, Dad," came a whisper from the head of the stumbling figure.

"I can't 'ear you, Colyn. Stop pullin' my flippin' lug'oles off!" hissed a voice from the depths of the cloak.

"Sorry, Dad." Colyn loosened his grip on his father's ears and promptly toppled from his shoulders.

The cloaked figure staggered blindly on for a few steps. "Oh, gorblimey," it lamented, "I've gorn and lorst me 'ead!"

Hearing the commotion, the other cloaked figure hurried back to the stricken pair. "Stop messing about," hissed Bertram. "You'll never get away with that troll disguise if you carry on like this." He helped Colyn back on to his father's shoulders. "I wish Humfrey was here."

"'E says he's got to keep an eye on what's happenin' in the City," said Colyn. "And anyway, you needed the best nickers in Dun Indewood fer this caper. And that's me and Dad."

They set off again through the gloom, heading to the flattened fields where the mighty troll army was encamped.

"Halt! Who goes there?" The challenge brought the two cloaked figures to an abrupt halt. A suspicious-looking guard was approaching through the murk.

"Let us pass!" said Bertram in what he hoped was a commanding voice. "I've got an urgent message."

"Yeah? Well, I've got a big club with nails in it." The guard scowled. "So you can just stay there and tell me who you are."

"I'm..." Bertram searched his mind desperately. "I'm Dolerite Gypsum, and this is... erm ... Zircon Mudstone."

The guard looked "Zircon Mudstone" up and down. "You sure he's a troll? He's very thin."

"I've been ill," muttered the ex-King of Thieves.

The guard looked startled. "Why's he talking out of his stomach?"

"Wind." Bertram grabbed his companion by the elbow

and hurried the stumbling figure away. "Can't stop. Urgent message for General Moraine. Good to see you're on the alert. Well done." Bertram hurriedly ushered his lurching companion into the safety of the shadows while the guard stared after them, scratching his crest.

After this encounter, Bertram's heart pounded whenever they passed a patrol, but these guards merely nodded and grunted as the hooded figures hurried by. Confident of their superior strength, the troll forces clearly had no fear of attack. Soon, Bertram, Colyn and the ex-King of Thieves were in the camp itself, passing by tents and groups of trolls who sat around campfires; talking, joking and sharpening an array of weapons. Although he'd been away for many months, Bertram had never seen anything like this in Caer Borundum. Things have changed a lot, he thought to himself.

After much directionless wandering among the apparently endless lines of tents, Bertram found a quiet spot behind a supplies wagon. "This is hopeless," he hissed. "I'd no idea this camp was so big – we'll never find the Sceptre."

The ex-King of Thieves' head poked out from the cloak. "'Course we will," he said. "All we got to do is find this Granite geezer. He's not gonna let it out of his sight, is he?"

"And how do we do that?" demanded Bertram.

"Easy." Spotting a passing troll, the ex-King of Thieves gave a sharp whistle. "Oy, 'scuse me, mate!" he called, ignoring Bertram's frantic shushing. "Where's the General's tent?"

"Over there." The troll pointed vaguely into the darkness.

"Three lines across, four back. Big gold effort. You can't miss it." He wandered on his way.

"There you go, my son." The ex-King of Thieves patted Bertram's trembling arm. "You only got to ask. We know where the tent is; now we just got to get in there."

Bertram shook his head. "*I* need to get in there. You two will be spotted."

"So will you," said Colyn bluntly. "Didn't you say this General knows you?"

Bertram nodded glumly. "I'm afraid he does."

"Then you'll need a disguise." Colyn slipped down from his father's shoulders. "Leave it to me."

Before Bertram could object, Colyn had vanished into the dark.

The King of Thieves dropped the cloak and gave an appreciative chuckle. "Chip orf the old block, he is," he said proudly. "Don't worry. He'll be back soon."

And, to Bertram's amazement, before long Colyn *was* back – carrying a leather hood with eye-holes. Bertram turned the strange object over in his hands, puzzled. "What is it?"

"Dunno," said Colyn brightly. "Pinched it out o' some troll's pocket. Ugly-looking geezer, even for a troll. No offence." He grinned at Bertram. "Anyway, it's a disguise. Put that on an' even your own muvver wouldn't know you."

Bertram put it on. The hood covered his whole head down to his shoulders at the back, leaving only his nose and mouth free at the front. He had some trouble seeing out of the eye-holes, but Colyn was right – it was a good disguise.

"You wait here," Bertram said at length. "I'll see if I can find out where the Sceptre is. If I get the chance, I'll grab it – so be ready to run. All right?"

"All right," said the ex-King of Thieves.

"All right," confirmed Colyn.

"All right," echoed a voice from under the discarded thieves' cloak.

Bertram gave a start. "Cliff!" he hissed. "What are you doing here? You were supposed to stay with Luigi."

"And miss a near hundred per cent opportunity to get myself done in?" demanded the lemming, scrambling clear of the heavy folds of the cloak. "No chance!"

Before he could reply, a voice from behind them caused Bertram's stomach to turn in on itself. "You there! Yeah, you! Come here."

The ex-King of Thieves gave Bertram a nod. He and Colyn silently faded into the shadows. Bertram turned around – and gave an involuntary gasp. The voice calling to him belonged to Gabbro, one of the trolls who'd helped Granite throw Bertram over the falls.

"You're wanted!" Granite's henchman swaggered up to Bertram and prodded him in the chest. "General Moraine wants his chief interrogator – right now!"

Bertram fought to keep the panic out of his voice. "What makes you think I'm General Moraine's chief interrogator?"

Gabbro gave him a hard stare. "'Cos you're wearin' the chief interrogator's hood," he said. "Bit of a give-away. You windin' me up?"

"No," said Bertram hurriedly.

"Good. We caught a couple of deserters. The General wants you to get a confession out of them. Come on."

Gabbro led the way through the camp until they came to the General's great pavilion, made from cloth of gold and guarded by huge troll soldiers. The guards saluted Gabbro and stepped back, allowing him and Bertram entry into the tent.

Granite Moraine was standing in front of his throne. His face, lit only by two glowing braziers, contorted with fury as he pointed at the trembling troll kneeling before him. Bertram groaned inwardly as he recognised the General's victim. Opal's friend Clay was held in a vice-like grip by Granite's other bully-troll, Wolframite. Bertram had last seen Granite in Greystone Park. He had been laughing at Bertram then. He wasn't laughing now.

"You been very naughty!" roared Granite. "You dun a bad fing!"

Clay was snivelling with terror. "Please, General – we just wanted to go home. It don't feel right being above ground like this. We just wanted to go back to the mountain." Seeing no mercy in Granite's stony gaze, Clay pointed to another troll who stood pinioned by two guards. Bertram recognised another of Opal's friends – Greywacke. "It was all his idea!" squealed Clay.

His grovelling only increased Granite's fury. "Bad troll!"

screamed the deranged general. "Sneak! Traitor!" He raised his right hand.

Bertram gasped. In Granite's hand was a slender, golden rod, encrusted with precious stones and with a huge diamond set into its end. With a pounding heart, Bertram recognised the device drawn on the slate that Councillor Shale had shown him. The Sceptre of the Last Stygian Kings!

Tendrils of gloom roiled around the crystal. This was the heart of darkness – the weapon that had drained the sunlight from the sky and created the shadow over Dun Indewood.

Clay screamed and Wolframite hastily stepped back. Granite levelled the Sceptre until the crystal was pointing directly at his howling victim. The gemstone pulsed with power and the air around it crackled. Then, in an eye-searing blaze, the sunlight that the Sceptre had bled from the sky was released in one blinding burst of light. Every troll in the tent cried out and buried his face in his hands as Granite Moraine roared in rage and triumph.

When Bertram next looked, he saw Clay crouched on the floor, arms outstretched in a desperate and futile attempt to defend himself. But what had been a living, breathing creature was now lifeless and still – a cringing, pitiable figure of solid stone. Greywacke stood staring at the remains of his friend, his expression a mixture of pity, horror and fury.

One of the Granite's officers coughed apologetically. "Erm... perhaps you shouldn't have done that, General."

Granite spun to face him, his eyes glinting dangerously. "You sayin' I can't stone anyone I want to?"

"No, no," gulped the officer, backing away hurriedly, "I only meant, perhaps we should have asked him some questions before you stoned him – to find out if there were any other trolls involved in the conspiracy."

Granite glared. "I knew dat." Nevertheless, to the officer's obvious relief, the general lowered the Sceptre and placed it on a low stone table beside his throne. He turned his glare on Greywacke. "Bring de uvver one."

Wolframite and Gabbro seized Greywacke and forced him to his knees. Granite grunted with satisfaction. "Now then, pris'ner..."

Greywacke gave him a defiant glare. "You know my name, Granite."

The troll leader glowered. "Now then, *pris'ner,* you are goin' to tell me what I want to know." He beckoned to Bertram. "You – inter... introllo... you what asks the questions – get on wiv it."

Bertram gulped inwardly and stepped forward, glancing cautiously to left and right. As his gaze swept past Granite's shoulder, he almost stumbled as he caught sight of the tent walls behind the general. A knife, glinting dully in the light of the braziers, was industriously slicing through the canvas. Then three pairs of eyes appeared through the rip – one pair high, a smaller pair very low, and a third between them. Bertram's heart pounded. The ex-King, Cliff and Colyn! Now, if he could only distract the trolls...

Bertram took a deep breath and tried to imagine how an interrogator would go about questioning a suspect. He stood in front of Greywacke. "Right," he said nervously. "Erm...

now, I'm going to ask you a few questions, so if you'd be so kind as to answer them..."

"Questions?" growled Granite. "Let's just get on wiv the frets and torture!"

Threats? Torture? Bertram thought furiously. "Erm... if you don't answer my questions," he continued, "I shall be really, really cross. And I'm afraid I shall be forced to hurt you quite a lot."

Granite scowled. "*Hurt you quite a lot*?" he mimicked. "Wot you playin' at?"

"It's a new method of interrogation," Bertram said, improvising desperately. "It's called 'Good Troll-Bad Troll'."

Granite looked puzzled.

"You've been nasty and now I'm going to be nice," explained Bertram.

Granite's brow furrowed even more. "Nice? *Nice?* You ain't supposed to be *nice*. What's wrong with me bein' nasty an' you bein' even nastier?"

"Trust me, it will work. This will gain the prisoner's confidence. Won't it?" Bertram turned to Greywacke. "Won't it?" he repeated pointedly.

But Greywacke was so worked up with fear and defiance he was incapable of taking a hint. Ignoring Bertram, he stared Granite squarely in the eye. "You're mad, Moraine," he blurted. "Attacking humans is one thing, but now you're hurting your own kind. How many trolls have you stoned on the way here, just because they didn't want to fight? And now poor old Clay – he was your friend..."

"Shut it!" Granite struck Greywacke across the face. A crack like a rockfall echoed round the tent.

Outside, the ex-King of Thieves grimaced. "This is our chance," he hissed to Colyn as the general strode up and down in a fury, ranting, the Sceptre lying forgotten on the stone table. "I'll just nip in an' snatch the doin's..."

"What d'you mean, *you'll* nip in?" demanded Colyn in a hoarse whisper. "I'm littler an' sneakier than you, I'll go an—" He broke off and stared through the hole in the tent. "Oh, lumme," he said softly. "That's torn it!"

The ex-King of Thieves followed his glance. "Strewf!" He hissed as loudly as he dared, "Cliff! Don't be a wally! Come back 'ere, you muppet! Leave it alone!"

To his companions' horror, Cliff had sneaked into the tent and was now climbing on to the table where the Sceptre lay. As Colyn and his father watched, the tiny rodent struggled to lift the weapon, which was much too heavy for him.

"Hup! Ha! I've got it, I've got it, I've got it..." The Sceptre wobbled. "I haven't got it..."

The Sceptre slipped from Cliff's grasp and fell back on the stone table top with a crash. Instantly, every eye in the tent was on the panting lemming.

Cliff tried desperately to brazen it out. "Er... Sceptre Cleaning Services," he squeaked. "Special pick-up, as per instructions. We clean and polish all magical weaponry, a sparkling showroom finish or your money back..."

Granite may have been the most stupid troll in trolldom, but Cliff wasn't fooling anybody. With a bellow of rage that made the sides of the tent flap, the general snatched the

Sceptre and raised it to club Cliff into minced lemming.

"No!" shouted Bertram, stepping forward.

Granite swung round, his features twisted in rage. "Nobody tells me no!" he screamed. "You're gonna be stoned!" He ripped at the hood covering Bertram's face – and stopped dead in his tracks. The Sceptre slipped from his fingers and fell to the ground. "I killed you," he said in a cracked whisper. "You're dead!"

"Cliff!" yelled Bertram, "Colyn! King! Get out of here!" As his friends scuttled to comply, he dived for the Sceptre.

He was too late. With a curse, Granite snatched it up and aimed it at Bertram.

Once more the weapon pulsed. The air crackled. Bertram stood, rooted to the spot with horror. Another blinding, incandescent burst of concentrated sunlight swept over him, bathing every inch of his body with deadly, petrifying energy.

Chapter Seven

How Granite's Attitude Hardened, and the Attack of the Troll Lord's Army became a Monumental Fiasco.

The dreadful power of the Sceptre washed over Bertram. It was a strange sensation. Half of him felt as if it was being blasted by a force strong enough to stop the flow of blood in his veins, to still the beat of his heart, to tear the life from his body and petrify him where he stood. The other half felt as if it was being bathed in cold fire, racing and tingling along every nerve, making him feel more alert and more alive than he had ever been before.

Then it was over. The energy from the Sceptre flared and died. Bertram blinked – and realised that he was still there. Still alive. Still moving.

Granite stared at his enemy with a disbelief that was almost comic. He looked at the Sceptre and shook it, as if that might help. Then, with a bestial snarl, he aimed it at Bertram once again.

Bertram ducked. Behind him, Gabbro and Wolframite took the full force of the discharge. With the dreadful cracking noise of cooling lava, the general's luckless lieutenants were frozen for ever in the aggressive postures they had so often adopted in life.

Wide-eyed with terror, the remaining trolls gazed from their General to his stoned sidekicks and back again – then turned as one and ran, tearing right through the flimsy tent walls in their panic-stricken flight. Granite made no move to stop them. Bellowing with rage, he sent another Sceptre-blast towards Bertram's crouching figure. Bertram couldn't avoid it, but again, the light from the weapon had no adverse effect: it simply made him feel stronger, more powerful and more confident than before.

Slowly, Bertram uncurled and drew himself to his full height. His lips parted in a humourless smile. He looked Granite straight in the eyes and cracked his knuckles.

The troll general seemed to shrink within his golden armour. He gaped at Bertram, slack-jawed and empty-eyed. Then his arms fell to his sides and the Sceptre hung loose from his trembling fingers.

Bertram took a step forward. Granite took a step back. Bertram stepped forward again. Granite turned and ran. Caught off guard by his enemy's sudden retreat, Bertram hesitated.

"Bertram!" Greywacke was suddenly at his elbow. "You've got to stop him. He's gone crazy – he'll kill us all."

Bertram nodded. "I know. Find a weapon – anything!"

Feet churning the earth, he charged out of the tent in pursuit of his fleeing enemy.

Granite Moraine, Commander in Chief of the Armies of the Troll Lord, erupted from his tent. Fleeing from the terror of the despised troll who had returned from the dead to defy his power, he made for his war-chariot. Clambering on board, he held the Sceptre aloft.

"Guards!" he yelled in a cracked voice. "Guards! To me!"

Slumbering troopers blinked themselves awake and scrambled to their feet. Weapons drawn, they lumbered into position to form a defensive wall around the cart. Bertram emerged from the tent and skidded to a halt, faced with an impregnable wall of iron weapons and troll bodies.

From his position of safety, Granite Moraine regained his bravado. He brandished the Sceptre above his head and pointed a mocking finger at Bertram.

"You no-troll! You fing!" he jeered. "You fink, just cuz dis weapon don't work on you, you can beat me. But I got more dan dis!" He waved the Sceptre again. "I got a whole army!" He pointed a quivering finger at Bertram and screamed, "Kill him!"

There was no time to think. Everything seemed to happen in slow motion.

As the troops took their first step forward, Greywacke appeared carrying a shot for a siege engine. He lifted the smooth, spherical rock to forehead height and threw it with both hands – not at Granite, but in a looping trajectory towards Bertram, yelling, "Spike it!"

For a split second, Bertram was mystified: then he understood. Greywacke was treating the rock as a trolleyball. He was providing Bertram with a perfect, classic set pass.

Bertram gathered himself to leap, every muscle in his powerful troll body tense. The rock seemed to hang at the top of its arc, turning and tumbling slowly. Then it fell.

Bertram leapt and uncoiled his right arm. His hand, with all his enormous troll strength behind it, connected with the makeshift ball to send it rocketing towards the figure on the cart with a scream of tortured air.

Granite Moraine barely had time to register his peril, barely time to open his mouth and give a despairing scream: *"Nooooooooooo...!"*

The ball smashed into the Sceptre of the Last Stygian Kings with incredible speed and irresistible force. With an ear-shattering clap of thunder, the weapon exploded, releasing all its stored energy in a one searing, deadly blaze of twisted light. Shards of iron rained down on the astonished trolls below; jewels flew like shrapnel. Granite's howl died in his throat as it, along with the rest of him, petrified in a split second.

The trolls nearest the blast were turned instantly to stone and a clamour of alarm spread among the others. Bertram turned to high-five Greywacke – and saw to his horror that the young troll had been caught in the glare of the Sceptre's destruction and now stood, unmoving, caught for ever in the act of celebrating Bertram's success.

Silence fell. For a second, the entire host remained frozen. Then, slowly, fearfully, in one spellbound movement, the trolls looked up.

Above them, the shadow began to break.

Then there was pandemonium. Every troll in the vast army threw down his weapons and ran for shelter. Screams of panic mingled with howls of agony as slower trolls were trodden into the ground by others clambering over them in their haste to flee the deadly daylight creeping through the thinning gloom. Within moments, the great, invincible troll army had dissolved into a panic-stricken rout.

Many were too slow. Even as the front ranks crashed, howling, into the dense shade of the Dark Forest, the returning light caught the last of the stragglers. Bertram fell to his knees and groaned as he saw what must happen.

As the sunlight spread across the wreckage of the great camp, wave after wave of retreating trolls paused in mid-flight, stiffened, and toppled to the ground to move no more.

From the City walls came the sound of cheering, the peal of bells, the triumphant blare of trumpets. But Bertram fell to his knees, weeping for the fate of his stricken people.

With the sun blazing in a cloudless sky, the citizens of Dun Indewood emerged cautiously from the shelter of the city walls. Picking over the debris of the wrecked camp, they

exclaimed in wonder at the calcified bodies strewn over the ground. Almost a third of the great troll army lay petrified upon the abandoned field, while picksies wandered wretchedly among the unmoving figures of their former mining partners. With greasy troll-tears still streaming down his face, Bertram searched desperately for survivors – and found Marlstone, another of his former tormentors.

Marlstone was still alive, but in a bad way. He had almost made it to the shadow of the trees, but not quite: his bottom-half lay in the light, petrified into solid rock. A furrow stretching behind him showed he had tried to drag himself to safety. Marlstone was at the end of his strength and he stared at Bertram with exhausted, pain-filled eyes.

"You're dead," he grated. Then he gave a harsh bark of laughter. "Hey, what a coincidence! Me too!"

Bertram shook his head and took the dying troll's hands. He stepped behind Marlstone and pulled with all his might – to no avail. Even half a troll is a ponderous mass of rock to lift and Marlstone was bigger than most.

"Stay there!" Bertram told him, realising as he said it how foolish that sounded. "I mean, I'll get help."

Marlstone gave a harsh chuckle. "Poor old Bertie. Always looking for the happy ending." He reached out and grabbed Bertram by the shoulder. "Were you helping the humans?"

His face a mask of guilt, Bertram nodded.

"Good," said Marlstone unexpectedly. Bertram stared at him. The stricken troll gave a moan as the light crept further along his body. His voice was noticeably weaker as he said, "Us trolls have gone mad, I reckon. Granite stoned poor old

Clay, didn't he?" Bertram nodded again. "That's how it goes these days – for any troll who doesn't do as he's told..." His words ended in a groan as the light continued its deadly advance.

With a great effort, Marlstone went on: "You don't know how bad it is back home. The Troll Lord proclaimed that traitors would not be tolerated and soon folk began disappearing. Most of the Trollmoot vanished."

A cold hand clutched at Bertram's heart as he remembered the unseen voice by the falls: "*Soon, the traitors to trollkind will be dealt with...*"

"Councillor Shale?" he asked.

Marlstone nodded painfully. "He was the first..."

Bertram clenched his fists.

"Listen. You've got to go back." Marlstone's hand clutched at Bertram's arm with frantic strength. "Back to Caer Borundum. You smashed Moraine's Sceptre. You're the only one who isn't afraid of the power of the light. I thought you were soft and I was hard..." He gave a painful wheeze of laughter. "Yeah, well, right now I'm getting harder by the second. But one thing's for sure, you're the only one who can stand up to the Troll Lord..."

"Who is he?" Bertram shook Marlstone's stiffening shoulders. "Who is this Troll Lord?"

But though Marlstone tried to speak, the sunlight had crept relentlessly up his body. The last of the shadow fell away from the fallen body and Bertram found himself kneeling beside a block of lifeless stone.

"Hey, ma fren'!" Bertram raised tear-filled eyes to see

Luigi waddling towards him. The pastafarian's normally cheerful face was lined with worry. "We been lookin' all over for you. I was afraid you got turned to stone like the others!"

Unable to trust his voice, Bertram shook his head.

Luigi looked down at the stone figure. "Fren' of yours?"

"Not really."

"Ah, well." Luigi waved his hand. "Nasty business, ver' nasty. But i's over now, eh?"

Bertram gave Luigi a look that wiped the pastafarian's tentative smile from his face. "Many of my people are dead. Those that are still alive are in danger. The Troll Lord is undefeated and he still has a power greater than the one he has lost." He turned and seemed to stare, not at the stricken battlefield, but beyond it, across vast distances to the unseen troll mountain in the north.

"No," he said flatly. "It isn't over. It's just beginning."

Chapter Eight

How a Fellowship was Formed (just about).

"We have won a great and glorious victory against the forces of darkness!" proclaimed Lord Robat.

"Hear, bally hear!" agreed Sir Regynild le Bêtenoire. "We smote and smashed the sneaking, snivelling scum by force of arms!"

"The forshe of Bertram'sh arm," pointed out Humfrey, "with a trolleyball at the end of it." The boggart winked at Bertram. "Usheful game. You musht teach me how to play it shometime." Bertram nodded politely, though privately he thought Humfrey would have to be very athletic to make up for his lack of height. "Pardon me for shaying sho," the boggart went on, "but we've won a battle, not the war. That'sh why we're here."

Following the defeat of the troll army, Humfrey had demanded that Lord Robat call an immediate council. To avoid the endless bickering and arguments that constituted meetings of the Great Council, he had insisted that this gathering should be made up of a select few. The party that met in an upper chamber of the Citadel consisted of the Runemaster, Lord Robat, Humfrey, Bertram, Cliff (who hadn't been invited, but who was, as usual, hidden away in Bertram's pocket), Sir Regynild le Bêtenoire and Luigi (as commander of the City Militia and provider of light refreshments).

"Before we begin our discussion," said the Runemaster, "we must give thanks to Bertram for saving the City of Dun Indewood."

Sir Regynild grunted. "Sheer luck, if you ask me. Sneaking out of the City without permission. That troll camp was out of bounds, sir! Deuced ill-judged, idiotic, insubordinate thing to do. What would have happened if he hadn't managed to break the Sceptre, goodness only knows. If this feller were a Knyght I'd have his horrible, hideous hide horsewhipped for his foolhardiness."

Humfrey was prevented from giving the Head of the Knyght School a piece of his mind by the arrival of Colyn and his father.

"Sorry I'm late," apologised the ex-King. "Just been checkin' wiv the lads."

Lord Robat gestured the two latecomers to sit. "And what news do you bring?" he asked.

"I 'ad 'em doin' a sweep round the Forest to see if there's any trolls 'angin' about. There ain't – just a few statchers. The rest seem to 'ave scarpered. My guess is that they'll 'ide durin' the day and travel by night to get back 'ome."

"Then it would seem that the immediate threat has receded," said the Runemaster. "Yet it would be unwise to cease our vigilance."

"Yeah," agreed the ex-King, "an' we ought to keep an eye out for the devils an' all. No tellin' what they might get up to."

"Unfortunately," said the Runemaster heavily, "we have every reason to believe that we can tell exactly what the Troll Lord's next move is likely to be." He turned to Bertram. "Tell us about the two powers of the troll kingdom."

All listened intently as Bertram explained Councillor Shale's tale of the Orb and the Sceptre: that the Sceptre was a weapon to take into battle, but the power of the Orb was even greater. Bertram choked back a sob at the thought of Councillor Shale, Opal, his mother and what the Troll Lord might have done to them.

"What exactly is this Orb?" asked Lord Robat.

Bertram recalled the slate from Councillor Shale's study. "It's a ball of gold, covered in precious stones. The legends say that the Orb can darken the skies over the whole world for ever."

"Dam' deceitful drivel and nasty, noxious nonsense!" protested Sir Regynild. "Preposterous piffle and poppycock! Shadows yes, but a weapon that can cause everlasting darkness? Pah!"

"It is as Bertram says," interjected the Runemaster. "From my reading of the ancient archives, I believe that the Orb doth possess such deadly powers. But there is worse. The Troll Lord could use this Orb from within the very heart of the troll kingdom. He hath no need to expose himself to danger or his forces to further defeat. He doth not have to return to Dun Indewood with an army to threaten and fight us. He can use this ultimate weapon and achieve his victory from hundreds of leagues away."

"A conniving, cowardly codpiece!" thundered Sir Regynild. "What sort of a cheatin', churlish chicken is this Troll Lord? Not fightin'? What sort of spineless, splutterin', specimen of sputum doesn't want to fight?"

"The shame short who wash all for giving Dun Indewood to the trollsh and running away,' said Humfrey pointedly. "Now what shay you shush?"

As Sir Regynild turned purple and spluttered, Luigi held up a hand. "So why didn' 'e just use the Orb in the first place?"

The ex-King of Thieves nodded. "Yeah, why go to all that time and bovver wiv an army?"

"My guessh ish revenge," answered Humfrey. "It'sh a schtrange thing. Reashon fliesh out the window. It'sh the path to madnessh."

Bertram was once again reminded of the overheard conversation at the falls and the manic tone of the unseen speaker.

"Revenge indeed," agreed the Runemaster. "There is a warped satisfaction to be gained from causing thine enemies to realise their weakness, to savour the full bitterness of their defeat. Had the Troll Lord simply used the Orb to destroy the outerworld, we humans would not have understood the nature of, or reason for, our demise. By sending his army, the Troll Lord wanted us to know the cause of our defeat. To a mind like his, revenge is a dish best eaten while thine enemy looks on and starves."

"So what's he gonna do wiv this Orb thing then?" asked the ex-King of Thieves.

"If the Troll Lord uses his dreadful weapon, light will drain from the sky until the whole world is dark," answered the Runemaster. "Everlasting winter will come upon us. With no sun, we will freeze and die. And humans will not be the only living things to suffer. Every creature of the Dark Forest, every tree within it, every plant, animal and bird of the world above ground will die. Only the creatures of darkness will survive. To win the world for his people, the Troll Lord would destroy it."

The ensuing silence was finally broken by the ex-King of Thieves. "What a carve up!" he said indignantly. "Diabolical bloomin' liberty, that's what it is."

"This is truly grievous news," agreed Lord Robat.

"Indeed it is," said the Runemaster. "And those of us gathered here bear a heavy burden. The task of this council is to decide what we should do to prevent the Orb from being used."

There was a solemn silence as all considered the task ahead. At length, Luigi spoke up. "While we's thinkin' about it, anyone fancy a slice o' pizza?"

Humfrey rapped sharply on the table. "How can you think about food at a time like thish?" demanded the boggart. A thoughtful look crossed his face. "You got pepperoni with that?" Luigi nodded. "Anchoviesh?" Luigi nodded again. Humfrey shrugged. "Good call. I'm shtarving."

When Luigi's pizzas had been reduced to a few empty cardboard boxes littered with crusts and discarded olive stones, the Runemaster returned to his theme. "We must seek a final end to this threat. Whilst this weapon exists, all those who live above ground are in danger. We must not only defeat the Troll Lord, but we must destroy the Orb."

Lord Robat nodded. "Very well. Our task is to put the trolls' weapon beyond use – but how exactly are we going to do it? Send the Knyghts? Or the City Militia?"

Sir Regynild choked as a piece of anchovy that had lodged in a tooth cavity went down the wrong way. Luigi involuntarily rammed a toothpick into his gum. Both stared at Lord Robat in horror.

Humfrey shook his head. "An army ish out of the queshtion. Our only chance of pulling thish off ish through shecreshy and shtealth."

Luigi nodded enthusiastically. "Secrecy an' stealth. Tha's exactly wa' I was goin' to say. You don't want no armies trampin' about getting in each other's ways an' makin' the Forest untidy."

"Hear, hear!" agreed Sir Regynild, mopping his face with a dirty handkerchief.

"We gotta take the fight *to* thish Troll Lord," Humfrey continued, jabbing a finger on to the table for emphasis. "An' we gotta go in fasht an' hard. It'sh a groat to a gold crown that ash shoon ash he learnsh of the defeat, he'll use the Orb shtraight away."

"Humfrey's right," said Bertram unhappily. "If one of the trolls sent a carrier-bat back to Caer Borundum in all that panic, we may already be too late. We can't afford to wait. We must get to the Troll Lord first. We must fight him and we must win."

In a voice almost too low to be heard, the Runemaster said, "But who will challenge the Troll Lord in the very seat of his power?"

Bertram gave a resigned sigh. "I will. Besides, I have to find out what has happened to my mother and Opal and Councillor Shale."

The Runemaster raised his eyes and gazed steadily at Bertram. "Thy offer is truly heroic," he said. ("And truly stupid," Sir Regynild muttered under his breath.) "However, thou canst not go alone. Thou wilt need a group of brave and trustworthy companions. A small group of determined comrades to go with you to Caer Borundum. A group to represent all the free peoples of Dun Indewood."

"I'll go!" squeaked a voice from Bertram's pocket.

Bertram rolled his eyes and hauled the lemming out. "Cliff! You're not even supposed to be here!"

"Well, I am here," snapped the lemming, "and I volunteer."

"There will be untold dangersh," warned Humfrey.

"Exactly," said Cliff, with a show of bravado. "Sounds like just my sort of quest." But the lemming had been subdued since his reunion with Bertram among the statues of the battlefield and his voice was less cocksure than usual.

Lord Robat rose to his feet. "Then I shall decide which companions Bertram shall take with him. Within this room there are nine of us. This companionship of nine shall travel to the troll kingdom, overcome the Troll Lord and destroy the Orb." Lord Robat was suddenly seized with a coughing fit. "Ahuh! Except of course that my poor state of health makes it impossible for me to go. Besides, I have the City to rule. I would give anything to be part of this adventure, but alas!" The High Lord gave an almost-convincing sigh of dismay. "It is simply not feasible."

Humfrey raised an eyebrow. "OK, sho that leavesh a companionship of eight..."

Sir Regynild shook his head. "Sorry. I'd love to help you out, but I can't do it. I've got the terrible, ticklish task of the term's timetable to thrash out. Dam' difficult, devilishly devious job, no one else is up to it, blast, bother and blow my bally bad luck."

Humfrey stared at the Knyght School Headmaster with narrowed eyes. "Sheven..."

"Scusi," piped up Luigi. "I gotta run the restaurant..." Humfrey's lips pursed. "...an' the City Militia, of course," the pastafarian added, not quite quickly enough.

"Shix..."

"I don't think the leader of the Badgers should go," pointed out Lord Robat. Colyn bristled, and would have interrupted, but the ex-King of Thieves gave his son a sharp dig in the ribs with his elbow and nodded sagely, trying not to look relieved. "We'll need some enforcement around the city in case the trolls who escaped the battle try a sneak attack – otherwise who knows what you'll come back to? If you ever *do* come back, of course," the High Lord added thoughtlessly.

"True, Your Lordship," agreed the ex-King. "An' I couldn't possibly 'ave my nipper goin' wivout me. So, no Colyn either."

"Oh, Dad," moaned Colyn.

Humfrey drew in a deep breath. "All right, already! A company of four then. Myshelf represhenting the boggartsh, Bertram for the trollsh..."

"And humans. Remember I'm half and half."

"...trollsh *and* humansh. The Runemashter for the wizardsh..."

"And me for the lemmings!" Cliff struck a not-entirely-convincing heroic pose.

Humfrey closed his eyes. "It'll take a miracle."

"Jolly good, then, that's settled," said Lord Robat briskly. "So off you all go, defeat the Troll Lord, destroy the Orb and come back soon."

"Isn't there a problem?" All eyes turned to Bertram. "How will we get to Caer Borundum? It took me and Cliff months to get through the Forest – and I'm not even sure of the way back."

The gloomy silence that followed this was broken by screams of panic from the guards on the roof. There was a sudden flare of light from outside; a moment later, the room was plunged into deepest shadow.

"It's the bally Orb!" cried out Sir Regynild, ducking swiftly under the council table. "We're too late!"

But it wasn't. Humfrey led the charge to the roof where terrified guards scurried for shelter as two dark shapes dropped from the sky and landed deftly on the flagstones. The roof of the Citadel was once again bathed in late afternoon sunlight.

Bertram stared wide-eyed at the huge winged beasts standing before him. "Are they d-d-dragons?" he stammered.

Humfrey nodded, grinning. "One hundred per cent pure winged lizard. Accept no subshtitutesh."

The Runemaster held up his hand. "I greet thee, Greywing, Dragon of the Ragged Mountain."

"Thy messenger, the Whizzard Tym, told us that thou hadst need of us," boomed the larger of the two dragons in a voice that echoed from every tower of the Castle. ***"And I have heeded thy request, for thy people once did great service to dragonkind."***

"As thou didst to humankind," replied the Runemaster. "I thank thee for answering our need." He gestured towards the second dragon. "I see thou hast a friend."

"I am not the outcast I once was," said Greywing loftily. ***"This is Darkscale. She is my hoard-mate."***

The Runemaster bowed to Darkscale. "She too is welcome." Darkscale returned the greeting with a nod of her head.

"Thy messenger spoke of trolls. He said the city was beseiged, yet we saw no sign of such creatures as we

approached." The dragon stared pointedly at Bertram. ***"And yet ye have a troll amongst ye."***

Hurriedly, the Runemaster explained the events that had led to the meeting of the council and the decisions it had taken. The dragon hissed at the Runemaster's description of the Orb. ***"We dragons are creatures of the night, yet we value the day also. We would not wish for a world of eternal darkness."***

The Runemaster frowned. "We had looked for the return of our messenger with thy coming, yet our Whizzard does not accompany thee."

Greywing shook his great head. ***"When he left us, Lord Tym went straight to the country of the gnomes to seek their aid in your struggle."***

"Shame," said Humfrey, "His shpeed would have been an asshet in sheizing the Orb."

"It seems ill luck dogs us," sighed the Runemaster.

The dragon flapped his great wings. ***"It appears ye hast much need of haste. Therefore, we will carry ye swiftly to the kingdom of the trolls."***

The Runemaster bowed. "We thank thee." He turned to the others. "Collect your belongings. Luigi – gather together provisions for our journey. We leave within the hour."

As the sun dipped behind the horizon in the west, the companions gathered together in the courtyard.

Wiping a tear from his eye, Luigi helped the Runemaster and Humfrey climb on to Darkscale's back before passing up several bags of supplies. "I put in enough pasta for two to three days," confided the pastafarian, "an' some extra hot chilli peppers for the dragons, in case their fire goes out. Look afta youselves, huh?" Luigi went on tearfully. "Cos if ya don' come back, I'm gonna be mad at you!"

Bertram, with Cliff tied firmly to his wrist with a piece of string (in case the lemming had any lingering ideas about attempting a parachute jump without a parachute) climbed on to Greywing.

"Oof! Thou weighest a ton," groaned the dragon.

Humfrey waved his hand in the air and gave a whoop. "Dragon'sh roll!"

Greywing and Darkscale flapped their mighty wings. Then they surged upwards into the night sky, taking the companions towards the mountain and into the shadows of the Troll Lord.

Book The Third

The Book of Bertram

(The Return of the Thing)

Chapter One

How the Back Door was Blocked, the Boggart was Baulked and the Lemming was Nearly Baked.

Fires glowed across the barren slopes of Mount Ynside.

Bertram, clinging tightly to the hard ridge-scales of the dragon's neck, stared down gloomily as Greywing spiralled around the mountain, gliding with silent wings on the thermals created by the troll fires. The slopes of the mountain were pocked by small delves: crude holes and rockpiles which Bertram guessed must serve as daytime shelters for the guards that patrolled ceaselessly below them.

The sun had already been sinking when Greywing and Darkscale had flown over the last trees of the Dark Forest. Darkness had fallen as the dragons sped over the lonely moors. Now there was only the mountain, beneath which lay the city of the trolls. It loomed ahead, darker than the sky, a hunched, brooding mass of stone hiding an incalculable menace.

Below them, a flare-path of bonfires revealed a great scar running across the moors. It stretched to the very slopes of Mount Ynside.

"What's that?" wondered Bertram. "A landslide?"

"It appears to be a road," answered the keen-sighted dragon. ***"It leads to a mighty doorway in the side of the mountain. A roadway for the armies of the Troll Lord."***

"Bertram!" The Runemaster's voice, calling softly, reached Bertram's ears as Darkscale sideslipped closer to her mate. "Guide the dragons to the ledge thou used to venture in and out of the mountain. That will be our way to enter the troll kingdom."

Bertram's ledge lay just below a tear-shaped snowfield. Even in the darkness it wasn't too difficult to spot. But as the dragons glided in closer, Bertram gave a cry of dismay. His 'back door' had been obliterated. The grassy banks and bright flowers were buried beneath thousands of tons of tumbled rock and scree. There was nowhere for the dragons to land. They swept away from the mountain and settled on the moors, keeping watch on the distant fires while their riders conversed.

"It looksh to me," said Humfrey thoughtfully, "like shomebody wantsh to keep ush out."

Bertram gave him a startled glance. "It might be just a landslide."

"A very convenient landslide," said Cliff drily, "for a Troll Lord who doesn't want any unexpected visitors." The lemming gave Bertram an accusing stare. "I thought you said that entrance was secret."

"It was!" exclaimed Bertram. "I didn't tell anyone where it was except my mother and Councillor Shale and Opal..." Bertram broke off. His eyes widened in horror. "That must be it! The Troll Lord found out from them. He probably used torture..."

"Sheer shpeculation," Humfrey said harshly. "Anyway, there'sh no way of knowing, and nothing you could do about it if you did until we get inside." Bertram bit his lip and nodded. Humfrey tugged the Runemaster's cloak. "Sho. Whatsh plan B, Runey? Do we knock on the front door and shay 'Hi there, we jusht dropped by to tell the Troll Lord that hish army hash been shtoned'?"

"What about the way we came out?" squeaked Cliff. "The tunnel that leads to the secret cave behind the falls?"

Bertram shook his head. "No good. We'd be stuck in the middle of the Trollenbach Falls. No way up and no way down, unless you don't mind going *splat* on to the rocks below."

Cliff said, without much conviction, "*I* don't mind..."

"But the resht of ush do," snapped Humfrey. "Sho shut up."

"Anyway, there's..."

"I shaid, pipe down, rodent."

"But you don't understand," Cliff persisted. "This is important. There's..."

Bertram groaned. "Cliff, will you just be quiet?"

"Right," bristled the lemming. "If that's what you want, I'll *be* quiet. I won't say another word. You won't hear a peep out of me. I'll be as silent as the thing I'd be in if you didn't stop saving my life when I don't want you to. I'll be..."

"Shut up!" snapped Humfrey, Bertram and the Runemaster together. Cliff sulked.

"There is another way," said the Runemaster finally. His voice was low and hesitant, as though he was unwilling to speak but could not remain silent. "But it is dangerous. There is a path that leads to the lower levels of the troll kingdom. A forgotten shaft on the eastern slopes of the mountain leads to the city of Caer Borundum by way of the deepest underground passages."

"The deep levels?" said Bertram. "Nobody goes there. That's where the salamanders live. Councillor Shale was always having trouble with them sending lava flows into his mineshafts. They're very dangerous."

"I was not proposing to set up house," said the Runemaster sharply. "It *is* possible to venture though the realm of the salamanders."

Humfrey eyed his partner narrowly. "How do you know all thish?"

The Runemaster waved one hand vaguely. "I read it in the runes."

"Ish that sho?" Humfrey's eyes were no more than slits.

The Runemaster glared at the boggart. "If we wish to rescue the councillor," he said peevishly, "then we must be bold. It is our only chance to defeat this Troll Lord."

There was a considered silence. Finally, Humfrey gave a shrug. "I guessh you're right." He raised his voice. "Hey, you dragonsh!"

"We heard ye." Greywing's voice was mutinous. ***"What do ye think we are, door-to-door delivery dragons?"*** Nevertheless, it bent its foreleg to allow Bertram and Cliff (who was still sulking) to scramble on to its back. Darkscale did the same for the Runemaster and Humfrey.

The moon rose. Under the Runemaster's directions, the dragons glided in to a landing on the lower eastern slopes of the mountain. Their riders dismounted.

Greywing dipped his head towards the Runemaster. ***"Our task is done. Our size is too great to allow us to follow ye into the mountain."***

"Thou speakest true," said the Runemaster. He bowed low to each dragon in turn. "But for your aid thus far, we thank ye. Fare ye well."

Just then they heard confused shouts below them. The trolls left to guard Mount Ynside seemed from their voices to be mostly old or very young: Bertram had been right in his guess that most of the trolls of fighting age had been in Granite Moraine's army. But the guards had evidently spotted the dragons and weren't prepared to let their presence go unchallenged. Greywing and Darkscale took off, swooping contemptuously over the watchfires. Trolls danced with rage, brandishing spears and shaking their fists.

While the dragons diverted the guards, the Runemaster hurriedly guided the companions to a small cleft, overgrown with thorn bushes. Pulling his cloak around him for protection, he stepped into the bushes, beckoning the others to follow him. The cleft led to a narrow gorge, at the end of which lay a dark opening into the mountain.

"Our way to Caer Borundum," said the Runemaster, "and a perilous road. We must take only what we need: torches, water, a little food and this..." The old wizard reached into his sack and pulled out a bottle containing a white liquid. He uncorked it, splashed some on his hands and began to rub it on his face.

"Lava lotion," he explained, passing the bottle around. "Factor twenty-five. Rub it well in. It will help to protect ye from the effects of the heat we shall encounter. Be sure to rub some on your ears," he added. "People always forget their ears..."

Humfrey, grimacing, rubbed the mixture over his bulbous nose and offered the bottle to Bertram, who shook his head. Troll skin was supposed to be impervious to salamander heat. In theory. For a while.

The Runemaster muttered a few words. A tiny ball of light, like a Will o' the Wisp, appeared over his head. "This way," he said, and stepped into the tunnel. His companions followed and passed into the darkness.

On the other side of the mountain, the silhouette of a bat appeared against the rising moon.

A young sentry at the recently constructed gate of Mount Ynside looked up. "Here!" he cried. "What's that?"

His companion shielded his eyes. "The bat-signal, you fool." As the tired creature gave a dozen flaps of its aching wings and fluttered down towards its destination, the older sentry hurried to the bat-cave, arriving just in time to meet the new arrival. He fumbled awkwardly at the carrier-bat's leg, cursing at the creature's flapping wings, before removing the attached message.

As the bat flapped wearily to its roost, the sentry inspected the moleskin scroll, his lips moving as he read the hastily scribbled direction. Then he lumbered out of the cave and down the stone steps.

The young sentry met him at the gate. "Did you find the bat?"

"Yes," said the older sentry. He drew himself up importantly. "It had a Very Important Message from the army. For Lord Slate."

His companion was impressed. "Go on! I never knew bats could talk."

The older sentry gave a low chuckle. "Oh, nice joke, very good. I'll have to use that myself sometime."

"What joke?"

"The joke that... forget it, just open up the gate."

The great gate of Mount Ynside creaked open. The older sentry stepped through and hurried towards the Hall of the Mountain King with his fist clenched tightly around the Very Important Message.

Down and down the companions travelled, into the very heart of the mountain. The Runemaster led the way, his flickering magic light barely penetrating the all-encompassing darkness. The group travelled in silence, each member lost in his own thoughts. Bertram found the going especially difficult, the narrow rocky passages causing him to bend low and squeeze through as best he could.

After an age of walking in darkness, it began to grow lighter. The air became warmer and, despite the lava lotion, sweat began to form on the travellers' brows. The walls of the tunnels glowed red.

The Runemaster came to a halt and extinguished his light with a gesture. "There are flows of molten lava just beyond these tunnel walls," he said. "We must be nearing the realm of the salamanders."

At the same moment, Cliff gave an agonised squeak. Bertram realised that his friend was alight. He picked Cliff up and patted and blew frantically at his smouldering fur.

"Ooh! Eek!" complained the lemming. "Careful with the heavy handling!" The squeaks continued until the Runemaster saved Cliff from further damage by dousing him in lava lotion. The dripping lemming stood on Bertram's outstretched palm, trembling with fury. "Oh, thank you very much!" he snarled. "Now I'm singed *and* sticky."

"If you can't be grateful, be quiet." Bertram stuffed the

protesting rodent into his pocket. "And don't come out."

The Runemaster tore a strip from the hem of his cloak and began wrapping it around his hands. "Even with the lotion, our skin will burn if we touch the rocks," he told Humfrey. "Bertram's skin should be protection enough, but not ours, alas."

Humfrey nodded and sacrificed the sleeves of his jerkin.

They set off again, taking care not to touch the walls. The tunnel was wider now and the heat more intense. Humfrey tiptoed gingerly along the passage. The heat from the ground was even starting to penetrate the soles of his boots now and the temperature was almost unendurable. The relentless heat made him feel as if his skin was on fire and his lungs about to melt. Beside him, the Runemaster was clearly having similar difficulties. Bertram felt pity for his fellow travellers. "Warm work," he said, giving them what he hoped was an encouraging grin.

As the tunnel opened out into a huge cavern, Cliff poked his nose out of Bertram's pocket. "Are we nearly there yet? Can I come out now? It's like one of Luigi's pizza ovens in here." The lemming blinked and looked around. "Wow! Impressive!"

The cavern's great jagged walls, glowing red and yellow, reached up to a roof that shimmered in waves of heat and dripped sparks of fire. Small holes peppered the walls, giving them the appearance of cheese that had been attacked by hungry mice.

As they carefully avoided the streams of sparks, Humfrey suddenly stopped and held up a warning hand. "Can you feel shomething?"

"What?" asked Bertram.

"Short of a shakin' – more a tremblin' – short of a..."

"Look out!" Bertram dived at Humfrey and dragged him to one side. Next moment, a pit yawned open where the boggart had been standing, shooting out tongues of fire.

"That wash closhe! Oooh!" Humfrey scurried forward, just avoiding another scalding jet of smoke and steam from a vent in the cave wall. "You know what?" said the boggart in a shocked voice. "I think shomething'sh trying to cook ush."

"What sort of something?" asked Bertram.

Humfrey pointed to a ledge. "Shomething like that."

The Runemaster and Bertram turned. A bright red lizard was gazing at them with yellow eyes that burned with incandescent rage. It seemed to glow, like a hot coal fresh from the fire.

"A salamander," breathed the Runemaster.

Cliff sniffed. "*That's* a salamander? I thought it'd be taller."

"What are you doing in our realm, cold creaturesss?" the salamander demanded, in a voice that hissed like spit on a hot stove.

"We do not mean to trespass," replied the Runemaster. "We seek only to pass through thy country. We wish to reach the city of the trolls."

"Oh, yesss? Oh, yesss?" The little lizard vibrated its tail angrily. "Ssso you sssay!"

"It's the truth, hot head!" snapped Cliff.

The lizard turned its hateful gaze to the lemming. "Are you talking to me, freeze-face? Are you ssstarting sssomething, chilly-chopsss?" It danced about in rage. "You come bursssting into our mountain as if you own the place! Oooh, you're really burning me up! Come on then! Let's sssee what you're made of, ice-featuresss! We'll make things warm for you! Come and have a go if you think you're hot enough!" It darted into one of the holes in the walls and disappeared.

The Runemaster and Humfrey leapt back as another split appeared beneath their feet and a tongue of fire shot out.

"Misssed!" The salamander stuck its head out of its hole and glared balefully. "Cursesss! Foiled again!"

The cavern floor grew even hotter. "The fire-lizards must be able to control the lava somehow," cried the Runemaster.

Bertram raised his voice and called out to the salamander, "Why are you doing this? What have we done to you?"

"It'sh no good!" Humfrey was hopping from one foot to the other as the temperature of the rocks increased. "Shome creaturesh jusht don't want to lishten. You ain't gonna talk it round. Fire'sh fire. It doeshn't care who it'sh burning or why: if you get in itsh way, you're burnt pizzsha, and that'sh all there ish to it."

"We'll all be burnt pizza if we tarry here!" The Runemaster narrowly dodged a blazing rock, thrown from a hole high above.

At that moment, with a great roar, a huge fissure opened behind them. A river of lava spewed out, pouring towards them.

"Going down!" Cliff dived back into Bertram's pocket.

Giving himself no time to think, Bertram picked up the Runemaster and Humfrey, tucked them under his arms, and sprinted across the cavern towards one of the tunnel mouths. The wave of lava raced along the chamber floor, lapping at his feet.

With a yell, Bertam charged down the nearest gaping tunnel mouth.

"This isn't the way!" yelled the Runemaster.

"Tell me about it later," Bertram puffed.

Behind him, the lava smashed into the wall of the cavern and exploded into thousands of small fireballs. Further down the tunnel, a red glow shone from a cleft in the wall. "Must be another cavern," gasped Bertram. "I'll head in there – we might be safer."

Unfortunately, they weren't. The diversion took them out of the path of the rushing lava, but as they emerged into the next cavern, a fiercer heat than any they had so far encountered blasted up at them.

Bertram backpedalled to a stop on the edge of a terrible gulf. His jaw dropped open. He set Humfrey and the Runemaster down. Cliff's head popped out of Bertram's pocket to take in the view. Trying to sound cheerful, the lemming said, "That's it! We're toast," and shot back into the depths of the coat.

Humfrey let out a low whistle. "Out of the frying pan..."

CHAPTER TWO

How Bertram suffered a Hot Reception and made a Promise, and Cliff had Second Thoughts.

By commandeering an elf-ant from the stables, the sentry had made good time in carrying the bat's message from the gates of Caer Borundum to the headquarters of the Troll Lord. He dismounted at the edge of the torch-lined ramp that led deeper into the mountain, to the recently excavated Hall of the Mountain King.

At the bottom of the ramp was a lobby. The ancient rock of the walls showed the scars of frantic digging. At its far end, several very large, black-uniformed trolls stood guarding a rust-pitted, ancient iron door. The Troll Lord's heavily armed personal bodyguards eyed the sentry suspiciously as he marched briskly to a marble desk, behind which sat a bespectacled clerk.

"I have a Very Important Message," announced the sentry. "A carrier-bat from our troops at Trollingrad has just arrived."

The clerk looked up. "What does it say?"

The sentry chuckled and gave a wink. "Nothing. Bats can't talk."

The clerk stared at him stony-faced.

The sentry began to panic. "I mean, they just sort of squeak – very high pitched, like this: *'Eeeeek! Eeeek!'* That's how they find their way about, you see, because their eyes are pretty useless. That's why it's safe to let them carry messages because they can't read and..." The sentry was silenced as the impatient clerk drummed his fingers on the desk, making dents in the marble.

"I meant," said the clerk in icy tones, "what is the content of the message?"

The sentry shook his head. "I can't tell you that. It's marked 'For Lord Slate's eyes only'."

"Then it will have to wait." The clerk waved a hand dismissively. "Lord Slate gave strict orders that he was not to be disturbed."

"But..."

"We have been waiting to take revenge on the human usurpers for thousands of years," said the clerk. "I'm sure that news of our wondrous victory at Trollingrad can wait a little longer." He gave the sentry a sly look. "However, don't let me influence you. If you are sure that your message is so vital that you will be forgiven for ignoring an express command from the Troll Lord himself to deliver it, go right ahead. It's your decision. Probably the last one you'll ever make," he added in a harsh whisper.

The sentry thought about the new 'statues' in Greystone Park. He thought about all the trolls who had disappeared, never to be seen again. He thought about the terrible wrath of the Troll Lord. He looked at the message, then glanced up at the door and the leering guards.

"Thanks, I'll wait."

Bertram and his companions stepped slowly back from the yawning chasm at their feet. Far below, raised stone platforms lay either side of a gorge through which a steady stream of lava flowed into a great lake of molten rock that gurgled and bubbled like boiling soup. There were salamanders everywhere, slithering along the stone walkways, swimming or diving into the lava lake. The multitude of red and yellow glowing lizards flowed over the naked rock of the cavern like living flames.

As one, the salamanders turned slowly and gazed at the companions with hateful malevolence. Cliff gulped. "I don't think they're very pleased to see us."

Bertram pushed Humfrey and the Runemaster behind him. "We can't outrun them," he said quietly, keeping one eye on the approaching fire-lizards. "They'll just keep sending lava flows after us and sooner or later they'll trap us in a blind passage. You two go. Keep climbing – the further up you go, the less danger from the salamanders and the closer you'll be to Caer Borundum."

Humfrey raised an eyebrow. "And what are you going to do?"

"I'm going to talk to them."

"Are you crazy? You think they'll lishten? You've got to be out of your..." But Humfrey's protests died away as the Runemaster gave Bertram a single nod of acknowledgement and, with unexpected strength, dragged the boggart away. They disappeared into one of the side tunnels.

Bertram turned to face the fiery chasm and stood quietly awaiting the salamanders. Cliff (whose fur had dried into spikes, making him look like a strange sort of hedgehog) gave the troll a worried look. "Just be careful, will you?"

"If I'm not," Bertram said tensely, "the salamanders will burn us where we stand."

"That's what I mean." The lemming eyed the fire-lizards apprehensively. "Despite previous indications to the contrary, when I go, I'd really prefer something a bit quicker and less painful than being burnt to a crisp."

The small lizards encircled Bertram. From a rocky ledge beside his ear, one, a deeper gold than the others, reared up and fixed Bertram with a baleful look.

"Creature of ssstone," it hissed, "cold-hearted enemy of my people, prepare to be incssinerated!"

"Oh, dear," said Cliff faintly. "Barbecue time!"

Ignoring the lemming, Bertram kept his voice level. "Why do you hate us?"

"Why? *Why?*" The salamander shook with rage. "You dare to ask thisss, when your minersss dessstroy our homesss, block our tunnelsss, kill our friendsss?"

"We don't do those things!" As he said the words, it occurred to Bertram that he wasn't in a good position to call the hot-tempered lizard a liar. Then he remembered what Councillor Shale had said about his deep-mining operations. With a great deal less certainty, he said, "Or if we do, I'm sure it was an accident..."

"Admit nothing!" hissed Cliff. "Claim diplomatic immunity..."

"Acsssident?" echoed the salamander balefully. "Acsssidentsss happen oncssse or twicssse. My people face death and dessstruction every day from the mining operationsss of the trollsss!"

Bertram thought quickly. Councillor Shale's miners were always complaining about the damage caused to their tunnels by the salamanders: but if the fire-lizards were under threat from the mining and simply trying to save their homes...

"Listen to me." Bertram looked the furious reptile straight in the eyes. "I'm sure the damage we've done to your people is a mistake. But whether it is or not, I promise you this. I am going to Caer Borundum to challenge the Troll Lord. And if I defeat him, I shall make sure that our mining no longer threatens your people. You have my word."

"The word of a troll!" sneered the salamander. Cliff closed his eyes.

Bertram shrugged. "If you burn me now," he said quietly,

"you will have a moment's satisfaction: but the trolls will continue to mine and more of your people will die. If you let me go, I can carry a message to my people and stop the troll miners." (I hope, he thought. If I manage to beat the Troll Lord – and if Councillor Shale is still alive – and if he listens to me...)

The salamander tilted its head to one side, considering. As if speaking to itself, it hissed, "Perhaps it isss worth the risssk." Then it raised its voice. "Very well. But tell your people thisss. If our realm isss further threatened, we will turn thisss mountain into a volcano and flood the tunnelsss of your city with molten lava. In order to do ssso, we will have to destroy our own homesss, and many of us will die. But we would rather die than sssuffer any further at the handsss of your people."

Bertram stared at the little creature in horror. He had no doubt that it could make good its threat. Dry mouthed, he said, "I shall tell them."

"Very well." The fire-lizard gave a series of commands in a voice like the cracking and spitting of a bonfire. The salamanders edged away, then slithered back to their chasm.

Bertram bowed to the golden salamander and, on slightly wobbly legs, headed for the cleft in the rocks through which Humfrey and the Runemaster had disappeared.

"Oh, blimey!" There was a tremor in Cliff's voice. "I thought we were gonners there."

Bertram stared at his spike-furred companion. "I thought you wanted to be a gonner."

"When you gotta go, you gotta go," said Cliff carefully. "But what I'm starting to think is, maybe I don't gotta go *just yet*."

"Do not fail usss!" The voice of the salamander pursued Bertram. He turned and nodded to the creature. They he stepped into the tunnel, leaving the realm of the salamanders behind.

Bertram continued through the miles of narrow passageways. Every so often he stopped to listen for sounds of Humfrey and the Runemaster, but the tunnels were silent except for the sharp plips of dripping water and the distant, echoing rumble of underground streams. Cliff trotted alongside him, silent and apparently lost in thought.

The companions stumbled blindly on. There was no light in these deserted passageways and Bertram had to fight against his fear of the darkness. He hoped that the others were still ahead of him and had not become lost in the maze of side tunnels. It was the main passage, he hoped, which would eventually lead them to the city.

Occasionally, the tunnel gave way to caves and caverns, their walls covered in glowing lichens which gave a faint, flickering light. Water trickled down moss-stained walls and the odd bat flew between the stalactites that hung from the yawning cavern roofs. At one point Bertram and Cliff had to cross a narrow stone bridge that spanned a terrifying abyss.

The rock was ancient and crumbling, and they edged across the gulf with the utmost care.

After what seemed like hours (and possibly was) they heard shuffling feet and a low, unhappy-sounding muttering from a cavern ahead. Cliff climbed up to Bertram's shoulder and whispered in his ear, "D'you think that's Humfrey and the Runemaster?"

"I don't know." Bertram tucked Cliff into his pocket. "If it isn't, it could be something dangerous. Keep out of sight."

In the dim light of glowing cave lichen, a thin, miserable looking troll was wading in a small pool of ankle-deep water, staring intently at its rippled surface. His hands were fumbling about under the water, apparently searching for something. Sensing Bertram's presence, the troll turned abruptly and stared malevolently at him with bulging, luminous eyes.

Bertram gazed at the strange creature curiously. "Who are you?" he asked.

"My name is Trollum," said the creature. Its eyes narrowed with suspicion. "You've found it, haven't you? Haven't you?"

"Found what?" Bertram was mystified. "I haven't found anything."

"Oh, no?" Trollum pointed a trembling finger at Bertram. "What have you got in your pockets?"

"A lemming," said Bertram. He took Cliff from his pocket and held him out for Trollum's inspection.

The small troll stared blankly at Cliff, who stared back. "Well, I'd never have guessed that."

"What are you looking for?" asked Bertram. "Can I help?"

Trollum shook his head unhappily. "I told my wife, 'If you take your ring off while you do the washing up, some day you'll knock it off the draining board' – but did she listen? No! And whose fault is it when it goes straight down the garbage chute? Mine, naturally! I've lost count of the days I've spent down here poking around for the wretched thing. I've not seen another living soul for years. I might as well be invisible."

"Why don't you just go back and tell her you can't find it?" asked Cliff.

Trollum gave him a hunted look. "You haven't met my wife, have you, my Precious?" Trollum gulped deep in his throat. "That's her name. Precious Stone. Very strong-willed, my wife."

Cliff whispered to Bertram, "We've got a right one here."

Bertram smiled at Trollum. "Can you tell me the way out of these tunnels?" he asked politely.

Trollum sighed heavily. "Search me. I lost my sense of direction ages ago." Without another word, the thin, sad troll bent its head once again to continue its fruitless search. Bertram and Cliff exchanged pitying glances and moved on.

Yet the sight of another living creature had raised Bertram's spirits. They rose further when, after another age of travelling through the subterranean depths, a sound reached his ears. A dull, distant booming noise reverberating through the rock.

"That sounds like the Trollenbach River," said Bertram. "We *must* be on the right track. All we need to do is head towards the noise."

Cliff still seemed rather subdued. "Whatever you say."

With every step Bertram took, the booming got louder until it was almost deafening. He felt his way along the tunnel that soon opened up into a cavern, filled with thousands of rocks and boulders. "This looks like an old mine," ventured Bertram. "And if it is, there must be some sort of exit."

Bertram peered into the darkness across the tons of waste rubble, searching for a way out of the depths. Then he spotted it. Above a small rocky ledge, a faint glimmer of light flickered. Bertram stumbled his way over the scree and hauled himself on to the ledge. There was a gap, just large enough for Bertram to squeeze through. He crawled along the passageway towards a shaft of light that shone down from a hole in the tunnel roof.

Squinting, Bertram peered upwards to the light's source.

"What is it?" asked Cliff.

"An air shaft," replied Bertram. "And our way out."

When Cliff had scrambled on to his shoulder, Bertram jammed his back against the side of the air shaft and braced his feet against the opposite wall. Slowly, he began to propel himself up the shaft as if he was climbing a chimney.

It was hard going. Bertram's muscles screamed at him as he pushed himself upwards. Cliff's exhortations of "Push, two, three; walk, two, three" had little effect on Bertram's determination to reach the top – the thought of his mother and Opal and Councillor Shale was sufficient to drive him on. Below, the rocky floor of the tunnel became more distant. Looking down, Bertram wondered what it was that attracted lemmings to long drops and hard landings.

After a long, agonising ascent, with a final push and scramble Bertram heaved himself out of the shaft and lay panting on the ground.

Cliff looked around. "What a dump."

Bertram recognised the mounds of spoil and abandoned machinery lit by dirty and broken glow-globes. "The old quarry works!" he exclaimed. "We're some distance away from the city, but it shouldn't take us too long to get there." Recovering his breath, he picked himself up and set off with wavering but purposeful strides, past a group of deserted outdelves towards a series of steps cut into the quarry wall.

Neither he nor Cliff noticed a dark figure sliding out of one of the ruined huts. Creeping towards the pair, it lifted a large troller hockey stick.

"Heeeeyahhhhh!" With a warlike screech, the assailant brought the stick smashing down on Bertram's head. Bertram blinked and staggered round to face his attacker. He gave a cry of astonishment.

"Opal!"

Then he passed out.

Chapter Three

The Rise of Slate, the Fall of Granite and an Unhappy Reunion.

"Ishpy," said Humfrey as he and the Runemaster trudged through the featureless tunnels, "with my little eye, shomething beginning with 'r'."

"Rock," said the Runemaster without hesitation.

"Right. Your turn."

"I spy with my little eye," the Runemaster said dully, "something beginning with 's'."

"Shtone."

"Correct."

Humfrey looked around at the tunnel walls, faintly glimmering in the phosphorescent glow of cave lichen. "Yep.

That sheemsh to have exhaushted all the posshibilitiesh."

Humfrey and the Runemaster had been walking for hours. They turned into yet another passageway that led to yet another gaping cavern. The Runemaster made an abstracted gesture and the light hovering above his head brightened momentarily. He looked around and shook his head unhappily. "I do not recognise this way."

"You keep shaying that," said Humfrey. "Like you've been here before or shomething."

The Runemaster coughed. "I meant that the runes have not foreseen this route."

"Right," nodded the cynical boggart. "Down here in the dark I shupposhe it'sh difficult to forshee anything." Humfrey stopped dead and turned to face the wizard, his clenched fists planted firmly on his hips. "Shee here, Runie, when do you plan to tell me whatever it ish you're not telling me?"

The Runemaster stared past the boggart's shoulder. "What's that shadow behind you?"

Humfrey clicked his tongue. "Tch, tch. Come on, Runie. That'sh the oldesht trick in the book."

"That *big* shadow...?"

"Yeah, yeah, yeah, and I shay 'What shadow?' and turn round, and you shay, 'I could've shworn I shaw shomething,' by which time I'm shupposhed to have forgotten the queshtion I ashked you that you don't want to anshwer..."

"There are three of them now," said the Runemaster. "Three big, *moving* shadows."

"Shure there are. Jusht how shtupid do you think I—?"

Humfrey broke off as a hand like a side of beef descended on his shoulder. He looked up into the leering face of a troll covered from head to foot in black, iron armour.

Humfrey turned back to the Runemaster and grinned weakly. "Oh," he said, "you mean *those* shadowsh..."

When Bertram came to, he found himself being smothered with hugs and kisses. The sensation was so unfamiliar and pleasant that it was some moments before he opened his eyes to find himself staring into the concerned face of Councillor Shale's niece.

"Bertram, Bertram, I'm sorry!" cried Opal. "I didn't know it was you! Are you all right?"

Cliff, watching Bertram's revival with an ironic grin plastered across his furry features, snorted derisively. "I told you he'd be all right. Thick skull for a thick troll."

Opal bridled. "Don't you say that about my Bertram," she chided.

Bertram shook his head, which felt as though it was about to float away. Had she really said, "My Bertram"? Surely he was dreaming...

"Can you stand? Let me help you. Can you make it to the building?" Opal tugged Bertram to his feet. Leaning heavily on her shoulder, he shambled to the shelter of the nearest crumbling workdelve on legs as wobbly as Luigi's best spaghetti.

"What happened to you?" demanded Opal, lowering Bertram to the stone floor as gently as she could. "I thought you were dead. I cried and cried."

Bertram stared at her. "Did you?"

Cliff sniggered.

"Well – a bit." A hint of her old defiance crept back into Opal's eyes. She lifted her head and made a bat-like chittering noise. An echoing sound came from behind a pile of rusting machinery and two more female trolls emerged hesitantly from shelter, gazing at Bertram with frightened eyes. His head still swimming, Bertram recognised Opal's friends Topaz and Garnet. Then Opal claimed his attention again.

"Where have you been? What are you doing here?"

With Topaz and Garnet listening, Bertram didn't feel like telling Opal the whole truth about his interview with her uncle, and his discovery that he was half-troll, half-human. Instead, he explained how he had been thrown from the Trollenbach Falls by Granite, and the story of his journey through the Dark Forest and his time in Dun Indewood.

"Dun Indewood!" Opal gazed open-mouthed at Bertram. "You were lucky you got out of there in time. Lord Slate's army is going to destroy it."

"Hah!" Cliff's shrill voice was scornful. "That's all you know..."

Bertram silenced the lemming with a look. "Who is Lord Slate?"

Opal shook her head. "Nobody knows."

"He always wears an iron crown that covers his face,"

Garnet cut in. "He says it's the crown of the Stygian Kings."

"And nobody's ever heard him speak," added Topaz, "except his officers. They give all the orders."

Bertram nodded and immediately wished he hadn't. "Tell me what's been happening here," he croaked.

Opal considered. "Well, your mother was frantic when you disappeared. She searched everywhere for you." Bertram bent his head in shame. "My uncle tried to help – he felt guilty about being the last troll to see you alive. He said that you'd been agitated when you left his delve." Bertram nodded again, more carefully this time. Opal went on, "The troll-wardens searched for you, but eventually they had to give up. They decided that you were dead or you'd left the troll kingdom for good."

Bertram gave a sigh. "I meant to."

"Then Slate appeared, calling himself the Troll Lord and claiming to have found the Hall of the Mountain King. People didn't believe him at first, but then he had himself crowned on the Obsidian Throne. The Trollmoot tried to stop him, but he had all the councillors arrested by squads of the TT."

"What are they?" asked Bertram.

Garnet shivered. "The Terror Trolls. Slate's secret police. They went round seizing dissenters and beating up anyone who was against the idea of war."

Opal nodded grimly. "My uncle was one of the first to disappear. Then, the day after the arrests, new statues started to appear in Greystone Park. Statues of some of the older members of the Trollmoot who'd spoken out against Lord Slate."

Cliff said, "We're not talking about sculptures here, are we?"

Topaz shook her head. "She means the real thing. They'd been turned into stone, as a warning to everyone."

"Was your uncle one of them?" asked Bertram nervously.

Opal shook her head. "No."

Bertram gave a huge sigh of relief.

"Not all the Trollmoot were turned to stone," Opal went on. "Some are still in prison – that's where Uncle is."

"And my mother?" asked Bertram anxiously.

Opal nodded. "I'm sure she is." She shuddered. "But some trolls were glad to see Slate take over everything: the ones who always think that everything bad that happens must be somebody else's fault."

Cliff scowled. "I know the type."

"Soon Slate's followers were on every street corner, ranting on about how we must take revenge on humans and claim back what is rightfully ours. Then Slate passed a law to form a great army. Thousands of young trolls joined of their own free will. The others were forced to join too, or thrown in prison. The mines and forges had to work flat out to make the weapons to arm the soldiers, but all the workers were in the army, so us girls were put to work in the mines and factories. But Topaz and Garnet and I escaped. We've been hiding down here ever since."

Opal gulped back a small sob, then continued. "We heard that engineers had cut a huge gateway in the side of the mountain and built a road that stretched across the moors, all in readiness for the army and their 'Just War' as Slate called it. And you'll never guess who was made general..."

"Granite," interjected Bertram.

Opal gave him a surprised look. "How do you know?"

"They had a reunion," said Cliff, "at Dun Indewood. You might say it was the highlight of the whole campaign."

Bertram had no choice but to tell Opal what had happened to Granite and the troll army. Then, watching Garnet and Topaz, he explained what Granite had done to Clay and what had happened to Greywacke and Marlstone. By the time he had finished, Garnet and Topaz were in tears.

Opal hugged them both in silence for a moment. Then she said, "I'm sorry for the others, but not Granite. He deserved what he got. Those who live by the stone, perish by the stone." She gave Bertram a sombre look. "So our army has been defeated?" Bertram nodded. "And Slate doesn't know that yet?"

Bertram shook his head. "Not unless he's received a carrier-bat from the army. He mustn't find out, because if he does, he will have no reason not to use the Orb. The Sceptre that Granite carried created a shadow over the troll army – but the Orb would draw the light from the sun and destroy all life in the outside world."

Opal clenched her fists. "Then now's the time to strike."

Bertram gazed at her in alarm. "What do you mean?"

Cliff closed his eyes. "I haven't even heard this plan yet," he said, "and I hate it already."

Opal, her eyes shining, ignored him. "Slate's army – or what's left of it – is straggling back from Dun Indewood. It won't be here for ages. Right now, there's only a bunch of old men and boys guarding the entrances to the mountain, and Lord Slate's personal bodyguard in the city. Don't you see, Bertram?" Opal grabbed his arm. "We can rescue my uncle and your mother. This is an ideal opportunity to overthrow the Troll Lord!"

Bertram was still arguing (in heated whispers) with Opal as they stood in Ironstone Square some time later. Bertram had been appalled by Opal's foolhardy plan to depose Lord Slate. He had tried to persuade her that they should find the Runemaster and Humfrey first.

"If they're still alive," Opal had pointed out, "and if Slate's guards haven't already found them, your friends could be anywhere by now! If you search all the tunnels below Caer Borundum, you'll never get to Lord Slate before he uses the Orb!" Bertram realised, with a heavy heart, that this made sense. He had agreed at least to listen to Opal's plan, but Topaz and Garnet, terrified at the prospect, had refused outright to have anything to do with it.

"But there are thousands of troll-women in Caer Borundum," Opal had argued. "We'd be more than a match for the men that are left if we all acted together."

"If!" said Cliff scathingly.

"But how can we contact the others?" wailed Garnet.

Topaz nodded sombrely. "Anyway, they wouldn't all be

on our side. Some of them believe Lord Slate's lies – and he still has the TT."

Opal fumed. "At least," she said, her eyes glinting dangerously, "we ought to try to get my uncle out of prison. People who wouldn't listen to us will listen to him."

Bertram grasped at this straw of common sense. "That's right. And my mother, too. Do we know which prison they're in?"

Grimly, Opal said, "They're where Slate puts all his prisoners. The Rock."

"The Rock?" Bertram gulped nervously. "But that's... I mean, no troll..."

"Yes, yes, yes," snapped Opal impatiently. "No troll has ever escaped from there. Think of it as an opportunity – we'll be setting a record."

Cliff rolled his eyes. "I should have jumped off that ledge when I had the chance..."

"All right," said Bertram helplessly, "I'll try and get in there and..."

Opal looked daggers at him. "What's all this '*I'll* get in there...'?" She seized Bertram's arm in an impressively vice-like grip. "We're in this together..."

"One for all," said Cliff mournfully, "and all for the chop!"

So they had set off, through a strangely altered Caer Borundum. There was little traffic and few pedestrians. The few civilian trolls were heavily muffled and scurried from place to place as if afraid of being stopped. They had good reason – trolls in black uniforms with TT insignia were everywhere, marching through the streets in squads, or simply standing staring suspiciously at every passing troll. Cliff remained out of sight in Bertram's pocket, to avoid attracting unwanted attention.

All over the city, there were posters: one had a picture of a grim masked figure saluting. Beneath it was written:

ONE LAND! ONE PEOPLE! ONE TROLL LORD!

Another had a picture of a troll soldier chatting to a trollwife. Two sinister-looking humans with big ears were listening greedily from behind her skirts. The poster read:

TITTLE-TATTLE LOST THE BATTLE!

YOU NEVER KNOW WHO MAY BE LISTENING!

CARELESS TALK COSTS LIVES!

A third poster showed a gloating human in robes (Bertram guessed he was supposed to be a wizard) with lightning shooting from his fingertips, laughing horribly as he turned a number of defenceless trolls (mostly women and children, who for some reason looked much smaller than the human) to stone. The caption to this poster was simply:

REVENGE!

Outside the Trollmoot hall a huge banner hung across the whole front of the building. It read:

GLORIOUS NEWS!
TROLLINGRAD RECAPTURED!

Bertram stared at it. "But that's not true!" he said.

"Ssssh!" Opal took his arm and dragged him away from a lounging group of TTs who looked as if they were about to take an interest.

"Well, it isn't," protested Bertram in a hoarse whisper. "The trolls were beaten."

Opal punched Bertram's arm fiercely. "Wake up, Bertram! Since the Troll Lord took over, nobody knows what's true and what isn't in Caer Borundum. Anyone with any sense just agrees with whatever Slate tells them – it's a lot safer!"

Now Bertram and Opal were standing beside the outer wall of the maximum security prison known throughout Caer Borundum as "The Rock", next to a very recent statue of a former member of the Trollmoot, who had seemingly annoyed Lord Slate and been too slow to duck. Opal was timing the movements of the guards patrolling outside the fortress. "Eleven... twelve... thirteen..."

Bertram stared glumly up at the sheer, solid ramparts carved from the living stone of the mountain. "What we need is a plan of the layout in there. Even if we got inside..."

"Ssssh!" Opal glared at Bertram. She continued her count: "Fourteen... fifteen... sixteen." Opal stopped counting as the guard reached the furthest extent of his beat and turned to face the opposite way with a complicated series of stamps and a lot of clanking. "That should just give us time to run across the square and hide in the shadow under the drawbridge. Then we have to wait, but not for long, because when they get back to the gate, the guards will turn again and march for sixteen paces..."

"Seventeen," said a voice behind them. "You lost count."

"Whoops!" said Cliff's muffled voice from Bertram's pocket.

Opal and Bertram turned very slowly. They stared at the black uniform with the shiny buttons stamped with the Orb and Sceptre of the Troll Lord. At the shiny mole-leather boots, gloves and belt. At the collar, with its TT insignia. At the hard, unsmiling face...

"Beryl!" Opal gave a gasp of relief. "Oh, Beryl!" She seized her old friend by the arm. "Thank goodness it's you!" A look of unease crept into Opal's eyes. "But what are you doing in that uniform? You haven't... I mean, you can't..."

There was no friendliness in Beryl's eyes. They were as bleak and merciless as the coldest glacier on the mountain. "Opal Drumlin!" she hissed. "Niece of the traitor Councillor Shale. We've been looking for you." She gave Bertram a scornful glance. "And Bertram Hornblende. Granite told me he'd dealt with you. He always was a fool. You won't escape me so easily."

Opal's eyes were wide and frightened. "Beryl," she pleaded, "what's wrong with you? You can't mean..."

Beryl broke Opal's grip and twisted her arm behind her. "You will come with me."

"Are you mad?" The pain snapped Opal out of her stupefied state. "You can't have joined Slate. He's a liar. He's evil. He's insane!"

Beryl stared at her for a moment – then one gloved hand whipped round in an arc, giving Opal a stinging slap on the face. With a shout of rage Bertram leapt forward – only to find his arms pinioned by two black-uniformed trolls. More trolls seized Opal as she staggered back. She struggled in their grip as Beryl stepped forward and thrust her face as close to Opal's as she could.

"Silence!" she screamed. "Shut your filthy, lying mouth. Lord Slate is our Great Leader! He is the saviour of the trolls! He will crush the human vermin beneath his iron heel!" Lowering her voice, Beryl hissed, "And for your information, Opal Drumlin, you will not address me as 'Beryl'. You are a fugitive and a renegade. And I am no longer the poor, silly girl who had to crawl on her knees to be allowed to be the friend of the high and mighty councillor's niece: though I was always better than you!" Her lips were flecked with spittle. "Always! Now, I am Major Beryl Loess of the TT and you will do well to remember that!" Raising her voice once again, she gave a crashing salute and cried, "One Land! One People! One Troll Lord!"

Her squad responded with ringing shouts. "One Land! One People! One Troll Lord!"

Beryl turned to her followers and pointed a black-clad finger at the forbidding gate of The Rock. "They are wanted for questioning. Take them away."

Opal's eyes blazed. "Ask away, Beryl. We'll tell you nothing."

"True." The TT leader's smile was terrifying. "You'll tell me nothing because I won't be asking the questions. You're to be taken to the Troll Lord." In spite of herself, Opal gave a gasp. Bertram's heart skipped a beat. Beryl's leer widened. "That's right. You are to be interrogated by Lord Slate himself!"

Chapter Four

How Bertram and Opal were Taken for a Ride.

The guards, using unnecessary force, thrust Bertram and Opal into a dark, rock-hewn cell. For a moment, Beryl's gloating face leered at them through the open doorway. Then the heavy iron door slammed shut and they heard the sound of a key turn in its lock. Bertram spun found and shoulder-charged the door in an attempt to force it open, but the trolls who had built the cell had known what they were doing. The door was massive and the rock surrounding it so hard that, even with a picksie to wield, it would have taken weeks to cut through it.

A flickering glow-globe set into the damp wall barely

pierced the gloom. Suddenly Opal gave a gasp. On the far side of the cell, hunched on a small stone ledge, was a figure shrouded in a black cloak. The figure stood, and drew back the hood shadowing its features.

Bertram and Opal cried out in unison.

"Uncle!"

"Councillor Shale!"

The old troll held out his arms. "My dear Opal."

Opal rushed across the room, flung her arms around her uncle and hugged him. Bertram looked on, feeling a stinging in his own eyes and a lump in his throat. He swallowed hard.

Eventually, the councillor extracted himself from his niece's embrace. "My boy; I thought you were dead." He clasped Bertram to his breast.

"You're squashing me," squeaked a voice from the depths of Bertram's coat. Councillor Shale looked surprised. Bertram took a step backwards and pulled Cliff from his pocket. Councillor Shale raised his eyebrows.

"This is Cliff," explained Bertram, feeling rather a fool. "He's a lemming."

"Nearly a lemming squash," grumbled Cliff.

The councillor bowed. "I am pleased to make your acquaintance, Cliff, although I wish it were in more pleasant surroundings and circumstances." He moved back to the ledge, sat down and patted the stone at his side. "Now, sit by me, Opal – and you, Bertram. I'm sure you have a great deal to tell me."

Bertram nodded. "But first," he said anxiously, "do you know what's happened to my mother?"

The councillor shook his head sadly. "I heard that the Troll Lord threw her into prison. Beyond that..." He shrugged. "I have no news."

Bertram clasped his hands together and said nothing.

"Now," said Councillor Shale briskly, "tell me all that has happened and how you come to join me in this sorry situation."

As he told his tale, Bertram examined Councillor Shale carefully. The old troll seemed to be in good spirits, though thinner and more haggard than Bertram remembered. Throughout Bertram's story, the councillor sat impassively, only occasionally nodding or shaking his head, until the young troll had begun his account of the siege of Dun Indewood.

"Tell me, Bertram..." The councillor's voice was low, but it trembled slightly, and he rubbed the fingers of one hand over the clenched fist of the other, as if struggling to maintain his composure. "What happened to the army? Was Trollingrad retaken?"

Bertram shook his head and explained how the battle had turned against the trolls.

Councillor Shale said nothing for a while. Then he gave a heavy sigh. "It is as well, perhaps," he said calmly. "Had he gained the victory, Lord Slate's position would have been unassailable. With the defeat of his army, we may yet hope that the Troll Lord too will fall – in time."

"But, Uncle..." Opal put her hand over the old troll's gnarled fist and gazed at him with anxious eyes. "We haven't got any time! Beryl said that we were to be taken to the Troll Lord."

Councillor Shale nodded slowly. "We must prepare ourselves for the worst and hope that others will continue the fight against tyranny."

Opal hugged her uncle again and burst into sobs. Bertram sat with his knees drawn up to his chest and thought bitter thoughts. He had seen himself as the big hero, coming to Opal's rescue; then forming a plan to rescue his mother and Councillor Shale: a plan of such genius that it would leave them breathless with admiration. A plan that would succeed brilliantly, leaving the guards gasping with bewilderment and the Troll Lord gnashing his teeth in impotent fury.

And what had Bertram achieved? He'd lost Humfrey and the Runemaster, and managed to get himself and Opal captured. He still didn't know for sure that his mother was all right, and now he, Opal and Councillor Shale were about to be taken before the Troll Lord, unless someone could suddenly think of a brilliant plan to save them.

"I've thought of a brilliant plan to save us," Cliff whispered in his ear.

"Have you?" said Bertram listlessly. "Oh, good."

"When they come to feed us, you stand behind the door, and when the guard comes in, you leap out and bash him, and pinch his keys, and bob's your uncle!"

Bertram gave Cliff a quelling look. "In the first place, I don't have an uncle. In the second place, I don't think they're going to feed us. And in the third place, the door opens outwards."

Cliff grimaced. "Those are problems, I agree." The lemming rested his furry chin on his paws in thought, then brightened up. "Right! Right! Got it. One of us pretends to be sick, see, and they lie on the floor going, *'Ooooh! Ooooh!'*, and when the guard comes in to find out what's the matter, we leap on him and..."

"What makes you think only one guard would come?" demanded Bertram. "How stupid do you think trolls are? Probably only one would come into the cell, we might be able to deal with him, but what about the half dozen or so waiting outside the door with big clubs? Anyway, why would they open the door at all? They're prison guards, not nursemaids. Why should they care if one of us is sick?"

"Ah, yes. Well, in that case..." Cliff clicked his fingers. "This one can't fail! What we do is, we start a fire, see? We make a lot of smoke and then..."

"...suffocate," supplied Bertram. "In any case, what are we going to start a fire with? This is a stone cell. It has an iron door. There's nothing to burn."

"Well, if you're just going to pick holes in every suggestion..." Cliff turned his back on Bertram and folded his paws. The cell fell quiet, the stillness broken only by Opal's sobs and Councillor Shale's mumbled words of comfort. Bertram brooded. Cliff sulked.

Bertram had lost all sense of time. It might have been many hours or only a few minutes later that a muffled clattering from the corridor outside signalled the arrival of their escort. At the sound, Cliff dived back into the relative safety of Bertram's pocket. The cell door cracked open and light streamed in. Beryl stood in the doorway.

Guards in TT uniforms thronged the corridor. Several of

them came into the cell, dragging its occupants roughly to their feet and hustling them out of the cell. Beryl issued terse commands while fixing Opal and Bertram with an exultant sneer. Manacles were produced and the prisoners secured. Craning his neck, Bertram gave Opal what he hoped was an encouraging grin. A jerk at the chain round his wrist made him stumble forwards. The escort moved off.

They marched through the silent, echoing corridors of The Rock: then out of its grim gates to a convoy of wagons pulled by draught-moles. Bertram, Opal and Councillor Shale were each led to a different cart. Once installed, they were further secured by chains leading to iron collars fastened round their necks. Bertram's was so tight he could hardly breathe.

The carts rumbled off through the dismal, almost deserted streets of Caer Borundum. They passed TT patrols, who saluted Beryl and shouted slogans and insults at the prisoners. They passed ordinary trolls who stopped what they were doing to watch the procession go by.

Then the convoy had moved out of the populated parts of the city and into a series of damp, deserted caverns. There was nothing to be seen beside the road now but mineworkings – not the orderly pit heads and workdelves of the industrial quarter, but scattered heaps of spoil, as if many test pits had been dug and abandoned. It was a bleak and tormented landscape, which only added to Bertram's depression.

At length, the carts came to a halt at the end of a long ramp lit by smoking torches. The prisoners and their escort disembarked, and set off down the slope, through a cavern hastily and unevenly gouged from the rock. A desk stood in the middle. Behind it, a small figure in spectacles was caught in the act of rising. Before it, a troll in guards' uniform stood frozen, cowering away from some danger. Both were petrified into solid stone.

Beryl tapped the smaller statue and gave Opal and Bertram a pitiless smile. "They delayed in delivering an important message to the Troll Lord." She shrugged. "They paid for their stupidity. As Lord Slate says, 'an example a day keeps the doubters at bay'." Beryl gestured towards the end of the cavern. "Now it is your turn."

Her gloved hand was pointing towards a gaping doorway. The ancient iron door, warped with age and streaked with corrosion, stood wide open. Twisted designs, cast into the metal, were made all the more horrible because time and rust had blurred their outlines into shapes as unclear as they were disturbing. A foul draught blew through the opening, smelling of age and cold decay.

Their escort fell back with apprehension. Clearly, even the hardened trolls of the TT stood in awe of the Hall of the Mountain King. Beryl said nothing, but her lips curled in anticipation as she gestured for them to go through the door. Bertram exchanged a hopeless glance with Opal, then squared his shoulders and moved forward. Councillor Shale put his hand reassuringly on Opal's shoulder and they all stepped over the threshold.

With a creaking, grating, rumbling sound, the door swung shut behind them, slamming into place with a great crash that made the floor tremble and shook the stone walls. They stood in complete darkness. Then a quiet hissing sound whispered through the cavern. With a series of small *whups*, gas jets at the base of the walls ignited.

Councillor Shale remained just inside the door, apparently taking in his surroundings. Opal moved to Bertram's side and took his hand. The two young trolls moved slowly away from the door, staring around in horrified fascination. Cliff scrambled out of Bertram's pocket and climbed on to his shoulder. He looked around and whistled.

They stood in a great cavern. Its walls, shimmering with crystals of all kinds, towered upwards, disappearing into a funereal blackness. Statues lined the walls: troll kings long dead peered disapprovingly down on the intruders who had dared enter their silent realm.

"Gloomy," said Cliff in a voice that faltered a little, "isn't it?"

Bertram gave him a quizzical look. "I thought lemmings liked 'gloomy'."

Cliff stared at the looming statues. "I'm starting to think 'gloomy' is overrated."

The cavern floor was shaped like a shallow funnel. A series of ridges ran inwards from the walls in what looked like concentric circles. The centre of the floor was a featureless slab of stone. At the far end of the hall stood a dais of adamantine rock, on which sat a huge, black, glass-like chair. The light from the gas jets gave it a translucent quality. A canopy, carved in the shape of a bat, hovered above the chair, adding an imposing air of malignant grandeur. Before the black, shimmering structure stood a marble pedestal. On this lay a ball of gold.

"The Obsidian Throne," whispered Opal.

Bertram, hardly daring to breathe, nodded. "And the Orb of the Last Stygian Kings."

Cliff gave a sniff of disapproval. "Tasteless," he said, wrinkling his nose. "Showy."

Bertram stared into the shadows behind the throne. "But we were brought here to meet the Troll Lord and the throne is empty. Where is he? Where is Lord Slate?"

A voice behind them – a voice that was familiar and yet somehow horribly changed, said: "I am here."

Cliff's fur stood on end. In a faint voice, he said, "Oo-er."

Opal and Bertram stared at each other like two dreamers who knew they were in a nightmare, but could not wake up.

They turned and spoke together.

"Councillor Shale?"

"Uncle?!"

Chapter Five

How Lord Slate stood Revealed, and Humfrey and the Runemaster Rolled in.

Councillor Shale strode across the cavern floor and mounted the dais. The frail, bent old troll suddenly seemed tall and strong. He turned, cloak swirling, and lowered himself on to the Obsidian Throne. His hands gripped the bat-head carvings at the end of its arms. His brooding eyes rested on Bertram and his niece, but he said nothing.

Opal was dumbfounded. "No..." she murmured as if the denial could alter what she saw before her.

But Bertram, watching his former benefactor, felt his disbelief evaporate like early-morning mist on the mountain. The figure sitting on the throne was no longer the urbane, courteous,. slightly self-important Councillor Shale he had known. He had caught a glimpse of the councillor's true nature when Shale had told him the history of the Troll-Man Wars: but at that time, he had been too upset to see its significance. Now, the guard was down, the mask was off.

The old troll sat on the throne with easy arrogance. His mouth, set in a hard line, held the promise of great cruelty. His eyes burned with the humourless energy of the fanatic. The figure before them was a stranger, menacing and dangerous.

At last, he spoke: "Behold the Hall of the Mountain King. Behold the Obsidian Throne of the trolls. I am no longer Shale. Shale is a sedimentary rock. Passive. Dormant. Yet it can undergo metamorphosis and emerge changed. Hardened. Toughened. Remade. A new beginning requires a new name. I am now Slate. I am the Troll Lord."

Opal gave a scream of despair that echoed round and round the mighty cavern. "NO!"

Cliff whispered into Bertram's ear, "You know how to pick your friends, I'll say that for you."

Bertram felt cold and sick with realisation. "It was you at the Trollenbach Falls," he choked. "You were in shadow, I only heard what you told Granite. You talked about revenge and how you would deal with traitors – but you're the traitor! You told Granite to kill me."

Cliff groaned. "*Now* he remembers..."

Opal stared at her uncle in horror. Lord Slate remained impassive. "Moraine. An incompetent," he said evenly. "He couldn't even hurl you to your death successfully." Slate's eyes narrowed. "You were a disappointment to me, Bertram."

Bertram was mystified. "A disappointment?"

"Yes. I hoped that, when I revealed your heritage, you would join me. But you ran." Slate shook his head. "You couldn't face the truth. Weak. You were always weak. You would have betrayed me."

"Before you turned half the Trollmoot to stone? Before you threw my mother in prison and sent Granite out with an army to attack Dun Indewood?" Bertram's eyes blazed. "If you call that betrayal, yes, I would!"

Cliff tugged urgently at Bertram's collar. "Don't you think you should go for a slightly more submissive approach? A bit of light grovelling wouldn't go amiss..."

"I don't understand!" cried Opal. "You were in prison. We found you there. Why...?"

"A necessary deception," said Slate, without apology. "A carrier-bat brought me news of the defeat of the Troll Army and the reappearance of Bertram Hornblende, but the message was garbled and incomplete. I needed confirmation – which you were kind enough to supply." There was no humour in the Troll Lord's smile.

"Another triumph for Bertram!" said Cliff despairingly. "The one piece of news you swore the Troll Lord mustn't find out, that his famous army is now the raw material for a rockery, you go and give him yourself!"

"You lied to me!" Tears streamed down Opal's face as she faced her uncle. "You let me think you were in prison, or worse, and all the time it was you who..."

"It was I," interrupted Slate, raising his head, "who reshaped the destiny of trollkind. It was I who wakened our people from their slumber. It was I who set them on the road to freedom."

"It was you," grated Bertram, "who sat safe at home and filled the heads of thousands of young, foolish trolls with lust for revenge and dreams of glory, and sent them to their death."

"Their death?" The Troll Lord sprang to his feet, his fists clenched and his face working with barely controlled fury. "The blame for that is not mine, Bertram Half-troll. It is yours! But for you, I should have driven the human vermin from Trollingrad. That defeat, those deaths, are on your head!" Lord Slate regained control of himself with a visible effort. "However, it does not matter. My ultimate victory is assured."

"You mean the ultimate victory of the trolls, don't you?" said Bertram softly.

The Troll Lord waved a careless hand. "It is the same thing."

"Yeah, right," muttered Cliff.

Ignoring the lemming, the Troll Lord continued, "When I invoke the power of the Orb, it will begin to drain light from the sky itself. From the sun, and moon, and all the stars; until the whole world lies in shadow. Then we trolls will venture out from our underground prison and once again rule the world."

"There will be nothing to rule," said Bertram. "All the humans of the city, all the creatures of the Forest, all the birds, trees and plants: all will be dead."

The Troll Lord shrugged. "There are inconvenient aspects to the plan, I admit."

Cliff whispered to Bertram, "He's nuttier than a nut tree hosting the squirrels' annual nut-collecting championship. Humour him."

"Unfortunately," the Troll Lord continued, "you have left me no alternative. Had my army succeeded, I would have no need to use the Orb. I should have had my revenge. The humans would have known what it was to be a defeated people. To know who had beaten them. To suffer the humiliation of surrender. I gave them a double-edged choice: give up that which they held dear or die. I believe they chose to give up the City." Slate laughed harshly. "It would not have mattered either way. My orders were for them to be wiped out whatever choice they made." Slate's laughter died. "But my army failed – thanks to you. Now you and your human friends will pay for that hollow victory."

Bertram shook his head. He took a step forward.

The Troll Lord regarded him with a humourless smile. "You still defy me?"

"I will stop you," said Bertram. "If I can." He took another step towards the Troll Lord and the Orb that rested at his side. He was younger than Slate. He would fight him for the Orb – seize it – destroy it...

"I am sure you would. But I regret," said the Troll Lord scornfully, "I cannot allow it."

Slate twisted one of the carved bat-heads on the arm of his throne. There was a click. The Hall of the Mountain King shook. Opal gave a cry of alarm; she and Bertram leapt for safety as, with a juddering and grinding of stone, a section of floor in the centre of the cavern dropped and slid aside. A red glow forced its way through the aperture. As the gap widened, tongues of flame licked around its edges, leaping from the lava pit that had lain concealed beneath the floor of the cavern.

There was another click. Slate had turned the bat-head on the throne's other arm.

The great door of the Hall opened. Rumbling, and striking sparks from the floor, a great, spherical iron cage was rolled in by Beryl's squad. The TT major stood grinning as her followers brought the sphere to a halt, revealing that it contained two prisoners who were forced to take stumbling steps to keep their footing as the cage was rolled forwards. Bertram looked more closely – and his heart failed him. "Runemaster!" His anguished cry rang through the cavern. "Humfrey!"

Beryl laughed aloud at his dismay. With a curt gesture, she dismissed her squad. Humfrey grinned wearily at Bertram. "How're you doin', big guy?"

Cliff peered at the captives. "Oh, there you are," he said dejectedly. "We've been worried about you."

The Troll Lord reached for the Orb and settled back on the black throne, toying with the golden globe. "I believe we have reached a situation known as a stand-off," he said. "You wish to prevent me from using the Orb. But I have your friends, and if you attack me, you must abandon them."

Bertram hesitated.

"Uncle," said Opal in a voice that was no more than a whisper, "you can't do this."

The Troll Lord ignored her. "Think, Bertram," he continued smoothly. "Will you compound your treachery? Can you wilfully destroy your people's last chance of freedom from the Man-curse? Will you condemn us to eternal exile while our enemies rejoice in our ruin?"

"Bertram." The Runemaster's voice was hoarse. "Listen to me. This troll has told you that the humans invaded the troll lands, that the trolls were wise, and kindly, and peaceful until humans rose up against them. He deceived you."

The Troll Lord sat bolt upright. "Still your lying tongue!" he snapped.

The Runemaster went on, "The truth is that in those early days, the trolls ruled all the people of the Forest – men, elves, gnomes, and the rest – with brutal savagery. They killed, burned and enslaved at will. They harried us to the point of extinction. All our peoples – all, Bertram! – would have died out, had not my ancestors discovered a spell to turn the tide, which you know as the Man-curse."

The Troll Lord's face was a livid, snarling mask of hate. "Slanders," he hissed. "Foul lies and distortions."

"We called for a truce," the Runemaster croaked. "We tried to make peace, but the trolls would not listen. Instead, they forged the Orb and Sceptre, and threatened to plunge every living thing into eternal darkness. A flying column of our forces managed to prevent their king using these terrible weapons, else he would have destroyed the world in mere spite at his defeat. We could have killed the trolls then. We had cause and the power. But we did not."

"Such generosity," sneered Slate. "Such forbearance."

The Runemaster ignored the interruption. "Instead we left them in exile inside this lonely mountain."

The Troll Lord recovered his composure. "And as the good, kindly, benevolent Councillor Shale I set myself, under cover of my mining operations, to find the lost treasures of my people, and use them to destroy the human usurpers. But you!" The Troll Lord pointed a hand like a talon at the Runemaster. "You who are so eager to reveal what you claim to be the truth, there is one truth that you shrink from revealing. One truth that bears on Bertram alone. Shall you tell him what it is? Or shall I?"

Humfrey, who had been listening in exhausted silence, shook his head uneasily. "Uh-oh. Here it comesh."

Opal stared from her uncle to Bertram, struck dumb with horror and misery. Even Cliff had fallen silent.

The Runemaster hung his head and said nothing.

"Very well." The Troll Lord turned to Bertram. "You know that you are a half-troll. You have a troll mother and a human father. Your mother is safe – for the moment." Bertram stifled a sob. "As for your father – he stands before you."

Feeling as though his heart had indeed turned to stone, Bertram looked to where Slate was pointing. He stared through the bars of the cage into the anguished eyes of the Runemaster.

Chapter Six

How Humfrey and the Runemaster went for a Spin, and how Bertram's Swim caused a Slate to Fall.

Bertram gazed wide-eyed at the Runemaster. "You – are my father?"

Opal looked bewildered. "What does he mean?"

"I'm a half-troll," Bertram said harshly. "Your uncle told me that my father was human. That's why I left Caer Borundum."

Tears welled in Opal's eyes. "Oh, Bertram..." She sank to the floor and buried her face in her hands.

"But I never knew *who* my father was." Bertram kept his eyes fixed on the old wizard who stood trapped in the great iron sphere, at the mercy of the Troll Lord. "Until now." He pointed accusingly at the Runemaster. "You came to Caer Borundum disguised as a troll. You met my mother. You..." Bertram choked, unable to continue.

"Do you still have faith in humans, Bertram?" The Troll Lord's voice was low and mocking. "Think of your childhood; think of all the misery you suffered through being only a half-troll. Who ran out on your mother, leaving you fatherless? Who caused you such grief?" Slate pointed at the Runemaster. "He did. And did he even tell you the truth when he had the opportunity?" Slate chuckled. "Poor Bertram. Deceived by those he trusted most."

Cliff swivelled his head to stare from Bertram to the Runemaster and back again. "Is he kidding us?" The lemming rubbed his eyes with clenched paws. "*He's* your father? I'd never have guessed. Mind you..." Cliff peered intently at the Runemaster. "Take away the beard, and a few wrinkles, paint the skin grey and inflate to three times the size... yep. There's a definite family resemblance."

Humfrey twisted himself in his cage to face the Runemaster. "You know what, Runie? When you decide to keep me in the dark about shomething, you make shure it's a doozie!"

The Runemaster shook his head. "I am sorry, Bertram. I feared thou wouldst not assist us if thou knewest the truth."

"You see, Bertram?" Slate's voice once more took on the gentle, confiding tones of Bertram's old friend and protector. "Do you need any further proof of human treachery?"

Bertram closed his eyes. The Runemaster – his father! All his life, Bertram had blamed his father for his mother's unhappiness and his own misery. And then he had discovered that he really *was* different, only a half-troll – a *thing*, as Granite had once called him. And when he had gone to Dun Indewood – had the Runemaster recognised him? The answer came to Bertram immediately. Of course he had! The wizard's moody silences, the fact that he could never seem to look Bertram in the eye... the old man had known straight away, and had he greeted Bertram as his son? No, he had stood by even when Bertram was arrested and said nothing. Slate was right. Humans couldn't be trusted.

"Join me," Lord Slate's voice went on, full of warmth and understanding. "You and I, together, can control the destiny of our people." Bertram gave an uncertain nod. The Troll Lord smiled triumphantly. "Good. Let us end this."

Then Bertram felt an excruciating pain in his right ear, bringing him sharply to his senses.

"Are you crazy?" Cliff was dancing around on Bertram's shoulder, beside himself with rage, his muzzle sticky with purple troll-blood. " I thought I had a death wish, but that's just personal – you've got one for the whole world!" Bertram's bewildered expression served only to incense the lemming further. "Stop feeling sorry for yourself," he snapped. "So your dad ran out on you. Big deal. So did mine." He considered for a moment. "Well, to be accurate, not so much *ran out* as *jumped off*..." Cliff tweaked Bertram's bleeding ear and pointed at the Troll Lord. "Now tell Mister Creepy there to make like my dad and take a long walk off a short ledge!"

Bertram shook his head to clear it. Then he nodded grimly and took another step towards the Troll Lord's throne.

Slate gave a wry smile. "Oh, well." He twisted the upper half of the Orb. Left – right – left – left again. Then he gave Bertram a look oddly compounded of triumph and apprehension. "So – it begins."

Bertram stood rooted to the spot. Surely, Slate had not activated the Orb and condemned the world to eternal darkness – just like that? It was impossible! Yet, as Bertram looked on in horror, the walls of the cavern began to glow. Opal looked up and gave a stifled scream. From all directions, the light of the sun, light that had never before penetrated this deep hall, seeped through the rock of the mountain and flowed through the still air of the cavern in ghostly tendrils before disappearing into the Orb. From her position by the door, Beryl gave a cry and cringed away from the light, though in this diffuse form it could do her no harm.

The Troll Lord raised the globe above his head. "The power of the Orb is unleashed. It will grow stronger with every passing moment. You cannot stop it. You cannot destroy it. Bury it, and even from the bottom of the deepest chasm it will continue to do its work until every glimmer of light is gone from the world!"

"Hey! Bertram!" Humfrey's voice broke through Bertram's stupor. "Forget what the creep shaysh! You got to get hold of that fancy gizmo and turn it off before the whole world sticksh itsh head under the blanket for keepsh! Get to it!"

Bertram started towards the Orb. The Troll Lord made a signal. There was a creaking, grinding sound from behind

Bertram. What now? Turning, he saw that Beryl was straining against the side of the iron sphere. It began to roll, gathering momentum with every second. Humfrey and the Runemaster were again forced to walk forward to keep pace with the movement of the cage.

"An amusement devised by our ancestors, the Last Stygian Kings!" roared Lord Slate over the rumbling of the sphere. "A means they devised to deal with their enemies. I thought you might find it – diverting."

Bertram seethed with anger – the Troll Lord was playing with his victims, making them run to keep up with the pace of the sphere, so as not to be tumbled around inside it like peas in a child's rattle. But Slate couldn't believe that this would stop him...

"Bertram!" Opal's voice was almost a scream. "The floor!"

For a moment, Bertram stared at her blankly. Then, with a wrenching shock, he understood.

The floor of the cavern was not cut into circles. It was a spiral. The iron cage would roll down the slope, round and round the hall in ever-decreasing circles, until it tumbled into the fire pit at its centre.

"What will you do, Bertram? Save your friends or follow me?" The Troll Lord gave Bertram an ironic bow and disappeared into the shadows behind the Obsidian Throne. The light in the cavern began to fade as the remaining ghostly wisps of sunlight raced in pursuit of the Orb as Lord Slate carried it deeper into the mountain.

The sphere was gathering speed, clanging as it bounced

on uneven parts of the floor, striking sparks from the stone as it rolled inexorably on. The Runemaster, robes held high, was gasping for breath as he raced to keep up with the speed of the cage. Humfrey's short legs were no more than a blur as he scampered like a hamster in a wheel.

Bertram gave a cry of horror and threw himself at the cage. The heavy sphere flung him aside easily and continued unchecked. Cliff picked himself up. "Hey, getting killed in pointless ways is supposed to be *my* thing, remember?"

Opal prised a rock from the cavern wall, and rolled it into the path of Humfrey's cage. The iron juggernaut crushed it to gravel. Beryl's mocking laughter rang through the hall.

"Theresh... nothing... you... can... do!" Humfrey's panting voice was only just audible above the thunder of the cage, which was gathering speed with every revolution. "Get... after... the... Orb!"

Cliff tugged at Bertram's trouser leg and pointed across the hall, to where Opal was pulling at the translucent black throne on its dais. "Hi, big fella! You want to go help the girlfriend?" Bertram stared at Opal. What did she think she was doing? Then he caught on and ran to help.

Beryl's laughter died. Only when the Obsidian Throne began to rock, did she realise what Bertram and Opal were trying to do. With an outraged bellow, she leapt forwards.

The cage was on its last few laps of the Hall, spiralling inwards and spinning faster as it swept towards the fire.

The Throne suddenly gave way under Bertram and Opal's attack and tumbled down from its dais, catching Opal a vicious blow on the thigh as it fell. Splinters smashed from it as it bounced over the uneven slope of the floor, coming to rest across the second last curve of the spiral.

Beryl threw herself at the precious relic of troll power in a desperate attempt to drag it clear – but too late. The cage careened into her at top speed, flinging her aside. With a despairing shriek, Major Beryl Loess of the TT disappeared into the glowing pit. Opal covered her face.

The cage hit the Throne, which cracked but did not smash. Humfrey and the Runemaster crashed against the curved iron side, then tumbled helplessly as, with an ear-splitting screech of tortured stone and metal, the cage ground on its way. It shunted the Throne before it, slowing all the time, screeching and grinding until, with a final shriek and in a cloud of stone dust, the cage and the remains of the Throne came to a shuddering halt – at the very edge of the pit.

Bertram rushed towards the cage. Tearing at the weakened bars with all his troll strength, he succeeded in releasing the Runemaster while Opal dragged the groaning boggart clear. Together, the young trolls half-carried, half-dragged their battered and bruised companions away up the slope. As they did so, the Throne at last gave way to the pressure of the cage. It shattered into a thousand glittering fragments, and the broken iron sphere tumbled to its destruction. There was a roar from the pit as consuming flames leapt up to the cavern ceiling.

"Bertram!" Humfrey hauled himself on to one elbow. "We'll be fine. Get after Shlate. Shtop him, any way you can, or it'sh curtainsh for ush all."

Bertram nodded and turned to Opal. She was rubbing her leg and grimacing with pain. Seeing Bertram's questioning look, she shook her head. "My leg's as stiff as a glow-post. I couldn't keep up." Her expression was pleading. "Bertram, remember, whatever he's done – he's still my uncle."

Cliff scrambled back on to Bertram's shoulder. "Is this the bit where we face certain death?" he asked apprehensively. "Or did I miss that part?"

Bertram took a deep breath. "I'd say there's still every chance."

Cliff sighed. "You know, this constant danger stuff is starting to get me down."

Bertram stared at him. "What's the matter? Do you want to live for ever?"

"Not for ever," squeaked Cliff, "just a bit longer..."

"Then you'd better hang on tight." Bertram raced up the slope, across the empty dais and into the shadows, following the Troll Lord and his deadly burden.

Bertram plunged into a rough-hewn tunnel and followed it, ignoring the battering he received from projections on its uneven walls. The Orb was obviously too far away for the daylight seeping through the mountain to be visible, so the tunnel was quite dark, and damp from the walls made it slippery underfoot.

As he ran, Bertram realised that there was a noise coming

from the tunnel ahead: it grew gradually from a dull rumble to a full-throated roar. In spite of his need for haste, Bertram began to slow down. Even so, he was unprepared for the sudden end of the tunnel and skidded to a halt, teetering dangerously at its mouth. Below him raced the foaming waters of the Trollenbach River.

Bertram groaned. "No wonder nobody found this way into the Hall of the Mountain King!"

Cliff, clinging on to Bertram's collar for grim death, said: "But Lord Slate must have come this way..."

Bertram pointed to an iron ring which had been hammered into the cliff beside the tunnel mouth. "He must have had a boat waiting for a quick getaway."

"Well, there's only one way to follow him." Cliff pointed at the raging torrent.

"There's a problem," said Bertram. "I can't swim!"

"This would be a terrific time to learn."

"I mean, trolls can't swim. We're too heavy."

"As you've pointed out several times, you're only half a troll."

Bertram stared at the tumbling, hissing flood below them. "So your theory is, if I jump into that, I'll only half-drown?"

Cliff sighed. "Look at it this way: if you don't stop Slate he'll plunge the world into eternal darkness and destroy everything above ground that matters to you. Do you really have a choice?"

Bertram gritted his teeth. "All right. I'll jump if you'll jump."

Cliff gulped. "After you."

"No, you go first."

"I insist. Don't forget to hold your nose."

Bertram took a deep breath. "Tell you what – both together. Right?"

Cliff nodded nervously. "Right."

Paw in hand, they jumped.

A long and horrible time later, Bertram found himself washed up on a sandbar. He was lying on his back, gasping feebly for air. His head hurt from the bashing that it (and just about every other bit of him) had received from rocks during his tumbling, headlong rush along the Trollenbach River. His stomach also hurt. It took him a few moments to realise that this was because Cliff was using it as a trampoline.

"What are you doing?" he wheezed.

"Trying to get some of the water out of you," said Cliff, bouncing furiously. "I tried giving you the kiss of life, but I fell in. Do all trolls have mouths as big as yours?"

Bertram brushed Cliff aside and rolled groggily into a sitting position, coughing up quite a lot of the river as he did so. "I swam," he said in wonderment.

Cliff gave him an ironic look. "If you can call it 'swimming' – more like 'delayed drowning' if you ask me."

Bertram couldn't argue. The frantic doggy-paddle he had adopted had resulted in his spending more time under the water than above it, but he seemed to have survived. "Where are we?" he asked weakly.

"Near the falls. It's a good thing we drifted inshore or we'd have been swept straight over."

Bertram shuddered. Not again! One trip over the falls was more than enough. He groaned. "Where's Slate?"

Cliff pointed further down the sandbar. A boat, carved from pumice stone, had been hauled up on to it. "I'd say he got here before us."

Bertram staggered to his feet. As he did so, he realised that their landing place was lit by a strange, diffuse radiance he had never seen before anywhere along the course of the river.

"That's the light going into the Orb," he said softly. "He must be very close."

As silently as he could, Bertram padded away from the river with Cliff following.

They found the Troll Lord standing on the ledge overlooking the Trollenbach Falls.

Holding the Orb aloft, Slate laughed as the sunlight seeped through the rock above and swirled into the voracious globe.

"Welcome, Bertram!" The Troll Lord could not have heard Bertram's cautious approach over the roar of the falls, but somehow he had known the younger troll was there. Giving up all attempt at concealment, Bertram stepped forward. Cliff remained lurking in the shadows, his tiny black eyes glinting as they gazed at the Orb. Then the lemming switched his attention to the bare rock of Lovers' Plummet, high above. Biting his lip, the lemming began to climb.

Slate gave Bertram an ironic bow. "I really must congratulate you. I did not think you'd have the courage – or the luck – to follow me here. However, since you have, I shall satisfy my curiosity on one point. Ready or not..."

He took one hand away from the Orb. With the other, he lifted it higher. His thumb appeared to press one of the jewels on its surface...

...and Bertram found himself lifted from his feet and slammed against the rock behind him by a concentrated pulse of light from the Orb. It was like being blasted by the Sceptre, but many times more intense and powerful. Bertram felt as if the light was penetrating his body and rippling round his bones, washing through every vein and artery; a sensation that was simultaneously painful and electrifying.

The flare from the Orb winked out. Slate laughed as Bertram staggered. "Bravo! No troll could have withstood that blast. Your human heritage does indeed grant you immunity from the weapons of light."

Bertram drew himself upright. The power of the Orb had re-energised him. Now, he could fight the self-styled Troll Lord and gain control of the Orb.

"Come no nearer!" Slate's voice was sharp. "I know what you have in mind, but it would be foolish. I have only to drop this over the falls and it will be beyond your reach for ever.

But it will not stop draining the light from the world." Slate gave a shout of triumphant laughter. "You are powerless, half-troll! You have lost!"

From above them came a high-pitched cry. "Geronniiimmmmmmmooooooooooooo!"

Cliff leapt from Lovers' Plummet and dropped like a stone. His carefully judged trajectory sent him hurtling straight at the jewelled weapon which Slate was still holding over his head. The lemming's feet slammed into the Orb. The Troll Lord gave a cry of shock and anger as it slipped from his fingers and bounced across the ledge to Bertram. Cliff smashed to the floor, where he lay stunned and winded at Slate's feet. With a snarl of vindictive fury, Slate kicked out. Tumbling helplessly, Cliff rose into the air – and with a final, despairing squeak disappeared over the edge of the falls, into the dreadful cauldron of swirling water and seething foam below.

"Cliiiiifffff!" Bertram gave a howl of rage. After all the times he had saved the lemming from his self-appointed fate, after all they had been through together – and now, Slate had sent the helpless creature to his doom. Uncontrollable rage welled through Bertram. He bent purposefully to the ground and grasped the Orb. Turning to face the Troll Lord, Bertram slowly extended his arm so that the dreadful weapon was aimed at his enemy.

"You would turn the Orb against me?" Slate's voice was mocking. "I wonder, are you troll enough to use it? Against Opal's beloved uncle? Against your mother's dear old friend?"

In reply, Bertram uttered a blood-curdling roar and

squeezed the Orb until his fingers ached. One of the jewels clicked – and a soundless blast of pure light flooded the vast cavern, etching its contours on Bertram's streaming eyes. The Troll Lord stood stock still, caught in the deadly flare of the stored daylight within the Orb. Bertram's face was set in a snarl, Opal's plea forgotten. The light would be racing through his enemy's body, turning it to stone. This was the end of the Troll Lord!

Except that, when the light from the Orb died, Lord Slate turned a savagely smiling face on Bertram and held his arms wide like a magician who has performed a successful illusion. Realisation of what this meant hit Bertram almost as hard as the charge of the Orb itself. "You're still alive. But the light from the Orb would turn any pure-bred troll to stone. So you..."

"Yes." Slate's voice was harsh. His lips twitched and his hands clenched convulsively. "I, too, bear the taint of human blood. I, too, am a half-troll."

"Is that why you helped my mother?" demanded Bertram bitterly. "And why you were kind to me?"

"When I discovered the truth about your birth, I hoped that you would become my disciple: that one day you would join me in my attempt to wipe out the stain of my contamination, to cut out the foul taint of human blood. I hoped you would be my heir." The Troll Lord shook his head. "But then I realised the truth. You were weak. You *liked* the abomination of the light. The contamination of humanity was too deep in you. When you chose to betray me, I knew you had to die."

Bertram's anger began to give way to pity. "I think," he said slowly, "that the manner of my birth is only shameful if I think it is shameful. I accept what I am. You chose to fight against one half of your own nature. It has made you mad."

"Perhaps." Slate's teeth pulled back in a snarl. Then he pounced.

The fight was brief. In spite of Bertram's optimism, Slate was heavier and stronger than the young troll, and fuelled by the desperation of insanity. A rain of blows drove Bertram back: Slate's flailing arms knocked the Orb from his hands. With a shriek of triumph, Slate leapt on the Troll King's weapon and held it aloft.

"Be as you choose!" the Troll Lord screamed, pointing a trembling finger at Bertram. "Live with the pollution of your tainted blood! I choose otherwise! I renounce the light! I discard pity and compassion! I cast off my humanity! I am a troll!"

Whether the Troll Lord, in his frenzy, touched the jewel that caused the Orb to discharge its stored light: or whether the ancient device itself somehow reacted to Slate's denial of his true heritage, Bertram never knew. He simply watched in horror as, following the Troll Lord's final words, the Orb flared again – and this time, Lord Slate's insane laughter died in his throat as the blood froze in his veins, his muscles locked solid and his skin calcified. When the light died, the Troll Lord was a statue.

The Orb dropped to the stone at its feet. Without living muscles to balance it, the statue of the Troll Lord swayed –

then toppled backwards, to disappear into the mists of the Trollenbach Falls. The crashing sounds of its destruction on the terrible rocks of the cataract echoed from the gulf for a few moments. After that, there was no sound but the pounding water.

Chapter Seven

How The Rock was Opened and the Curse Lifted, and what Happened Thereafter.

For a long time, Bertram stood gazing over the ledge into the torrent of the falls. The Troll Lord was defeated – but at a cost. Cliff's sacrifice had saved Bertram, but the lemming was gone. Tears trickled down Bertram's scaly cheeks.

"Poor beast," he said at last. "Still – it's what he would have wanted."

"I don't think so." A small, high-pitched voice rose from the region of Bertram's ankles. "I thought what he wanted was supreme power and the destruction of all other living things. I reckon he'd've regarded this outcome as, frankly, a bit of a disappointment."

Bertram looked down and gaped. "Cliff?! You're alive!"

The lemming was limping badly. His fur was bedraggled and one eye was closed, but he carried himself like a conquering general.

"I've decided to give up the whole death-wish thing," Cliff said haughtily. "I've come to the conclusion that there's no future in it – plus it hurts like anything!"

Bertram was still gawping at Cliff in total bafflement. "But – what happened?"

"I landed on the ledge under the falls where I met you," said Cliff matter-of-factly. "There's another tunnel that leads back up here."

"Another tunnel?" Bertram blinked. He pointed an accusing finger at the lemming. "Did you know about this when we met on the ledge?" Cliff nodded. "Then why didn't you tell me?"

Cliff smirked. "You didn't ask."

"And why didn't you tell any of us about it when the dragons brought us to the mountain and we were looking for a way in?"

"I tried to," said the lemming in long-suffering tones. "I seem to recall everyone telling me to shut up. Anyway, it's all worked out for the best, wouldn't you say?"

The question caught Bertram off-guard. "I don't know," he said slowly.

"Well, you got the sunlight-sucking thing, and the Troll Lord is starting a new career as gravel on a stream bed – I'd call that a pretty fair result in the circumstances."

Bertram's eyes narrowed. He drew himself up. "As far as

it goes, yes," he said firmly. "But there's more to do yet."

Cliff sighed. "Oh dear. You're going to be masterful now, are you, and save the world?"

"Yes," said Bertram grimly. "But first, I'm going to find my mother."

"Well, it's nice to see you've got your priorities straight."

"It's a long way back to the city," said Bertram meaningfully. "Do you want to ride or do you want to talk?"

Cliff scrambled up to Bertram's shoulder. "Mum's the word," he said. "Let's go and find her."

In the guardroom outside the main cellblock of The Rock, the roof and walls began to glow. The glow grew brighter. The TT duty officer rose from his desk and gazed at it in astonishment. Guards came pounding from their barrack delves to investigate. Somebody was bringing light into The Rock! Somebody was flouting the regulations! Somebody was going to suffer.

The light came from a strange round object, which was carried into the guardroom by a hard-eyed young troll with a small, furry creature sitting on his shoulder. The TT officer blinked – then remembered that he was supposed to be a leader. He pointed to the intruder. "Arrest him!"

Bertram held the Orb aloft. The guards who had moved in to capture him stopped dead in their tracks and stared at the glowing sphere with mounting alarm.

"The Troll Lord is dead," Bertram said quietly. "*This* is what killed him."

Cliff fixed the officer with a steely-eyed glare. "My friend is holding the Orb of the Last Stygian Kings, the most powerful troll-weapon in the world. Now, you may be thinking, perhaps there's not enough power in it to turn me to stone, and to tell you the truth, I'm not sure myself. So what you've got to ask yourself is: do I want to feel rocky?"

The squad backed off. Then, as one, the Troll Lord's guards turned and fled.

Bertram reached out as the officer tried to scuttle past him and grabbed the TT officer by the front of his tunic. "I want all the prisoners Lord Slate sent here released," he said quietly but very clearly. "Do it now. One of them is my mother."

The officer gave a panic-stricken nod and reached for the keys.

A crowd of trolls had slipped out of tenement delves and side alleys to follow Bertram as, carrying the Orb of the Stygian Kings, he had made his way to Ironstone Square. Now, the trolls gathered before the prison watched in amazement as the gates of The Rock opened. A rout of terrified guards tumbled out and disappeared into the streets of the city. Before long, as word of the Troll Lord's defeat spread, the gutters and wastebins of Caer Borundum were filled with discarded black uniforms. The trolls who had worn them were explaining that no, they had never been members of the TT, they must have been mistaken for somebody else, they had been away visiting sick relatives for a few months, and anyway they had only been following orders.

The crowd continued to grow. Picksies came to join it, wriggling through the forest of troll legs for a better view at the front. Something was going to happen. There was a sense of expectation in the air. Everyone gathered in the square was certain of one thing: they were about to see history being made.

It was to this vast, noiseless gathering that Opal brought the Runemaster and Humfrey, following the hurrying crowds and the glowing trails of light that seeped through the tunnel walls and sped towards the Orb. The light flowed across the square and through the walls of the prison, making the grim old fortress shine like a golden castle from the days of legend. They had barely reached the front of the throng that stood before the forbidding iron gates when the doors of the prison opened once more.

Trolls came out, male and female, walking slowly and hesitantly as if no longer sure their legs would support them: the survivors of the Troll Lord's reign of terror. All across the square, scenes of rejoicing erupted as the freed prisoners were greeted by family and friends. So it was that Bertram's reappearance with his mother went almost unnoticed, except by the Runemaster, Humfrey – and Opal, who gave Bertram's mother a quick, impulsive hug. Then she turned to Bertram with a look of desperate enquiry.

His voice faltering, Bertram told Opal what had happened to her uncle. Opal nodded, fighting back tears.

Bertram took his mother's hand and led her to the Runemaster. In an expressionless voice, he said, "I think you two know each other."

Pumice stared from her son to the Runemaster in bewilderment. Then she caught her breath. Something about this grave-looking human reminded her of a handsome young troll who had captured her heart, long ago. In a trembling voice, she said, "Malachite? Is that you?"

The Runemaster glanced at the crowd of trolls, listening attentively to every word. "Erm – dost thou think this is the time...?"

"It *is* you!" breathed Pumice. "You always used to say 'thee' and 'thou'..."

The Runemaster gave her an anguished look. "Wouldst thou not prefer to continue this discussion in private...?"

"I think there has been enough concealment," said Bertram. "Don't you?"

"As thou wishest." The old wizard drew himself up and spoke clearly, though he kept casting guilty looks at Pumice as he told his story. "During my wanderings in search of a lost treasure of Dun Indewood, I found myself near the mountain of the trolls. When I cast the runes, they told me that, one day, Dun Indewood and the whole world of the Dark Forest would stand in peril of its oldest and greatest enemy. I determined to visit Caer Borundum to see whether the tale of the runes was true."

"So you came to the mountain," said Bertram, "and met my mother."

The Runemaster nodded. "I used my magic to disguise myself and took the name Malachite." Pumice's eyes filled with tears. The Runemaster took her huge troll hand between his own. "I never meant to fall in love with thee, nor to cause thee hurt – but I could not stay. The spell had a limited life – and had I been discovered, thou wouldst have been in danger." The Runemaster hung his head. "I did not know that, by the time I left, thou wast with child." The old wizard turned to Bertram. "And when thou appeared in Dun Indewood," he continued, "though I guessed the truth, still I did not dare tell thee – for fear that thou wouldst turn against us, to the ruin of all." The old wizard closed his eyes. "I have done both of ye great wrong, believing I was acting for the best. I beg your forgiveness."

Pumice released one of her hands from the Runemaster's grip. She offered it to Opal, who, with a tremulous smile, reached out to Bertram, who in turn clasped the Runemaster's hand, completing the circle. In a voice that was only a little unsteady, Pumice said, "We all have a lot to talk about – and a lot to forgive." They stood in silence for a moment.

Then Bertram became aware that Humfrey was tugging at the sleeve of his jerkin, trying to get a word in edgeways. "Shorry to interrupt the touching family reunion," the boggart rasped, "but in cashe you've all forgotten, that Orb item you're holding ish shtill draining light from the shky outshide. Doesh anyone know how to turn the blashted thing off?"

The Runemaster nodded. "I have studied all that may be

learnt of the weapons of the Troll Kings. Yes, I know how to disarm it. But I cannot do so here."

From his position on Bertram's shoulder, Cliff eyed the wizard suspiciously. "Oh yeah? Why not?"

"The Orb would release all the sunlight it has stored from the outerworld in one flash of radiance. Every troll in the square would be instantly turned to stone." The crowd shifted uneasily.

Cliff nodded. "Good point."

"I must return to the world outside the mountain," the Runemaster continued. "Then the Orb can release its energies harmlessly." He held out his hands. "Give me the Orb."

Bertram shook his head.

Humfrey bristled. "What? Now, shee here..."

The Runemaster waved the indignant boggart to silence. He regarded Bertram closely. "What is thy wish?" he said at last.

"That you turn off the Orb here."

The crowd drew back. Cliff coughed warningly. "Er – Bertie, I think you may have lost the plot a little..."

The Runemaster looked nonplussed. "But I tell thee, thy people will die..."

"No," said Bertram. "They will not. Because before you turn off the Orb, you will lift the Man-curse."

A ripple of shock and horror, mixed with wild hope, spread through the crowd.

Humfrey marched up to Bertram. "Have you taken leave of your shenshes? Losht your marblesh? Lishten, kiddo, we're grateful for everything you've done here, including shaving our shorry backshidesh from that cage, but let'sh face factsh. It wash only a few daysh ago that a whole army of theshe guysh..." Humfrey waved at the surrounding trolls. "...came down out of the mountainsh with the expressh purposhe of shmashing Dun Indewood to shmithereensh. And they would have done it, too, except for the Man-curshe. And now you want ush to hand over the only protection we have againsht trollsh, jusht like that?"

"The only reason Lord Slate persuaded the trolls to go to war," said Bertram firmly, "was because of the Man-curse. Do you think there can ever be peace between our peoples while it remains in place?" Humfrey said nothing. "It seems to me a fair exchange," Bertram went on persuasively. "I saved your City. I offer you the chance to rid yourselves for ever of the most dangerous weapon my people hold against you. I ask in return that you remove the curse that has kept us in darkness for so long."

Humfrey glowered. "Looksh like you have ush over a barrel..."

Bertram shook his head. "I promised the salamanders I would stop the mining operations that were destroying their tunnels if they spared my life. They could have taken their revenge on me, but they let me go; and the mining *will* stop." Bertram took a deep breath. "My people have changed. Their exile has achieved its purpose. Your best guarantee of peace with trollkind is to remove the cause of their resentment against humans. Do this, and our people will live in peace. This is my promise to you."

There was a tense silence. Then the Runemaster gave a low chuckle.

"Thou hast the right of it – my son," he said.

Humfrey snorted. "Like father, like shon," he muttered. "I should have lishtened to my old ma – 'Never argue with a wizard,' she'd shay, 'unlessh you want to end up going green and living in the bottom of the well'."

The Runemaster ignored the grumbling boggart. He looked into Bertram's eyes, appearing to consider for a moment. The young troll met his glance steadily. Then the old wizard lifted his head and spoke so that his words carried to every last corner of the silent crowd. "Is it thy wish that, if the Man-curse is lifted, the Orb should be destroyed?"

There was a rumble of assent from the watching trolls. Bertram faced the Runemaster squarely. "It is."

"Then so be it," said the Runemaster simply. "Place the Orb on the ground between us." When Bertram had done so, the Runemaster beckoned to him, and to Bertram's mother. "Let us join hands in a circle. Troll, human – and thou, my son, who art both."

When the circle was complete, a hush fell over the crowd. Then the wizard closed his eyes and began to chant. He began in the High Speech, the ancient language of enchanters. The singing cadences of the old tongue rolled round the great cavern, awaking resonances in the rock that echoed back upon themselves, building until the thunder of words was as loud as the roar of the great Trollenbach falls.

At the last, the Runemaster threw back his head, and cried in words that all could understand:

"Man's ancient foes, deep-dwelling trolls with iron crowned
Thou hearts of stone, in gloom enthroned, in darkness bound:
Thy curse unmade, arise - avoid the shades of night
With these amends, thine exile ends. Behold the light!"

In the centre of the circle formed by the Runemaster, Bertram and his mother, the Orb glowed golden – then yellow – then white – until, on the last word of the Runemaster's incantation, it exploded, instantly releasing all its energies in a titanic burst of light. The trolls gathered in the square cried out and cowered away, shielding their eyes from such radiance as had never penetrated the dark halls since they had been hewn from the rock of the mountain, countless years before.

As the glow from that intense burst of light began to fade into the stones of the cavern on its journey back to the outside world, disbelieving trolls began tentatively to move limbs that, unaccountably, had not been turned to stone. They reached out and touched each other in wonderment. Light had come to Caer Borundum – and they were still alive!

And where the Orb had been, there was a slight scorch mark on the flagstone – and no other sign that the terrible weapon of the trolls, or the dreadful curse put on them by men, had ever existed.

And so it was that Bertram, with his mother and the Runemaster, Opal Drumlin, Cliff the Lemming and Humfrey the Boggart, led the trolls in a procession along the great road that Lord Slate had built for his armies. They followed Bertram through the echoing tunnels to the great gate in the mountainside. And, though it was full daylight, Bertram ordered the gate to be opened. The sun's rays streamed in, probing the secret tunnels, driving back the shadows.

The Runemaster stood back as trolls stumbled past him, blinking and shielding their eyes from the sunlight they had never experienced before. He felt a tug on his robes.

"Hey, Runie!" hissed Humfrey. "The mumbo-jumbo shtuff you did back there – level with me. Was all that shtrictly necessary?"

The Runemaster gave the boggart an austere look. "Art thou suggesting I was hamming it up? Stick to the inquestigating, Master Boggart, and leave the hocus pocus to me."

Humfrey gave the old wizard an sardonic grin. "Yeah, that'sh what I thought."

All around them, trolls were standing rapt with wonder at the blue of the sky, the stately dance of the clouds, the wheeling birds. Some knelt to touch, with trembling fingers, the sparse grass of the moors.

Cliff chuckled at the awed faces all around him. "It was about time you trolls lightened up and started to enjoy life. As I always say – look on the bright side."

Bertram stared at him. "Since when have you said that?"

"Since always, Mister Forgetful Troll! You know your

trouble? You need a more positive outlook. Every cloud has a silver lining. Here comes the sun. After the darkness, comes the dawn. What light through yonder window breaks? You are my sunshine, my only sunshine. The sun has got his hat on, hip hip hip hooray..."

"Cliff!"

The lemming gave Bertram a mischievous grin. "Yes, I know - 'shut up!'"

So ended the long exile of the trolls, and it was Bertram, the half-troll, half-human, who led his people as they took their first faltering steps out of the world of darkness and into the light.

Map of
Bertram & Cliff's
Journey to
Dun Indewood
Mount Inside
Bertram's
Ledge
Moors
The Sleeping Castle
The Ragged Mountain

The Sea
Gnorth Gnomedon
The Black Knyght
Ford
Sophie
Where Cliff met Wolfie
Great North Road
Dun Indewood
N

TALES OF THE DARK FOREST

KNYGHTMARE!

STEVE BARLOW & STEVE SKIDMORE

ILLUSTRATED BY FIONA LAND

Just when they think that the Dark Forest can't get any weirder or darker, Will and Rose start sharing the same nightmares. In a new adventure beyond their wildest dreams, even the mouthy Harp of Kings can't fathom this one!

"Schweet dreams sure ain't made of this!"
Boggart Tribune